THE CUTTING ROOM FLOOR

DAWN KLEHR

Woodbury, Minnesota

Indian River County Main Library
1600 21st Street
Vero Beach, FL 32960

The Cutting Room Floor © 2013 by Dawn Klehr. All rights reserved. No part of this book may be used or reproduced in any manner whatsoever, including Internet usage, without written permission from Flux, except in the case of brief quotations embodied in critical articles and reviews.

First Edition
First Printing, 2013

Book design by Bob Gaul
Cover design by Kevin R. Brown
Cover images © iStockphoto.com/9389095/mbbirdy,
5916995/Mlenny Photography,
15326086/DRB Images, LLC

Flux, an imprint of Llewellyn Worldwide Ltd.

This is a work of fiction. Names, characters, places, and incidents are either the product of the author's imagination or are used fictitiously, and any resemblance to actual persons living or dead, business establishments, events, or locales is entirely coincidental. Cover models used for illustrative purposes only and may not endorse or represent the book's subject.

Library of Congress Cataloging-in-Publication Data
Klehr, Dawn.
The cutting room floor/Dawn Klehr.—First edition.
pages cm
Summary: "When seventeen-year-old Riley Frost swears off romance and starts investigating a murder, she confides in her best friend, budding filmmaker Desmond Brandt, who may not have Riley's best interests at heart"—Provided by publisher.
ISBN 978-0-7387-3804-8
[1. Best friends—Fiction. 2. Friendship—Fiction. 3. Motion pictures—Production and direction—Fiction. 4. Sexual orientation—Fiction. 5. High schools—Fiction. 6. Schools—Fiction. 7. Murder—Fiction. 8. Mystery and detective stories.] I. Title.
PZ7.K678322Cut 2013
[Fic]—dc23

2013019723

Flux
Llewellyn Worldwide Ltd.
2143 Wooddale Drive
Woodbury, MN 55125-2989
www.fluxnow.com

Printed in the United States of America

For Leo

Acknowledgments

The Cutting Room Floor cast and crew are the best in the business and I'd like to take a moment to thank them here.

Roll credits:

The writer's support team: Sara Biren and Tanya Byrne. These two amazing writers have been with me since I started on this crazy journey and I would not be here without them. They were the first people to meet Dez and Riley and supported me every step of the way.

The incredibly talented agent: Jessica Sinsheimer, who believed in this story from the very beginning. Jessica asked the hard questions and did not stop until she got the best out of me. Her fingerprints are all over this book and I couldn't be happier with the outcome.

The stellar editor: Brian Farrey-Latz, who made this book shine. Extra thanks to Sandy Sullivan, Alisha Bjorklund, Mallory Hayes, and the entire team at Flux for all of your hard work!

The family: My husband, Lance, who immediately jumped on board when I told him I was going to write books and gave me the time, support, and love I needed to keep going. My son, Leo, who inspires me every day—his love of stories and fantasy makes me want to be a better writer. My mom, who is my biggest fan and continues to teach me lessons in patience—without which, I would've given up long ago. My sister Sara, who read all my early work and said she didn't just "like" it, she "loved" it. Way to build the confidence, sis. My sisters Julie and Libby, who are my cheerleaders and comic relief. My in-laws, Jim

3 2901 00579 1406

and Adrienne, who are never shy with their excitement and encouragement. I also have mountains of support from my brother-in-laws, nieces, nephews, and friends. Love you guys!

And finally, heartfelt gratitude goes out to the organizations that have helped me in so many ways: SCBWI, the Loft, and the MNYA writers: Liz, Ryann, Sara, Kari, Jonathan, Kitty, and Nikki. Thank you, thank you, thank you.

Fade to black…

In feature films the director is God;
in documentary films God is the director.
—Alfred Hitchcock

TITLE SEQUENCE

If my life were a movie, this would be the opening scene: a guy and his friend at the mall food court waiting for their dates to get back from the bathroom. I'm the guy, seventeen, somewhat troubled, sitting at a wobbly table with a plate of soggy nachos. This is my natural habitat. My natural, depressing, stifling, lame, pathetic habitat.

The title sequence would start out like a typical high school story, but then reveal that something's amiss. There'd be a tight shot, or piece of dialogue, or something that would make the viewer uncomfortable. Something to give them that prickly feeling. The kind that you feel deep in your gut.

Yeah, my life is *that* kind of story.

If I were Quentin Tarantino, I'd open the scene with all the players in my troubled life. We'd wear shades and walk down the streets of the Heights in slow motion, a gritty song playing in the background, just like in *Reservoir Dogs.* But I think my soundtrack would start with Chris Isaak's "Baby Did a Bad Bad Thing."

Or I could rip off the Coen Brothers. Start with a monologue where I wax poetic about life while showing scenes of my hometown, like in *No Country for Old Men.* I'd cut from shots of our old part of town with its decrepit buildings, vacant houses, and cars resting on cement blocks to the new area where homes sit on perfectly manicured yards and families ride to soccer practice in shiny SUVs. The haves and have-nots in our fourth-ring Twin Cities suburb. I'd throw in the clichéd Minnesota accent for good measure, since it worked so well in *Fargo.*

You betcha!

Or, if I were M. Night Shyamalan, I'd set up my opening scene in a creepy location—like the empty film editing suite in school—with eerie music playing in the background. But unlike in *The Sixth Sense* or *Signs*, there wouldn't be a supernatural element. *I* would be the cause of all the trouble. I'd call it *Desmond Brandt*, since it's *my* story. No. No, wait. It'd have to be about the girl. It's always about the girl. Yes, I'd call it *Riley Frost,* since it's her story too.

Most importantly, I'd have to show my character's redeeming qualities right away. Show that despite my narcissism, I really do care about others. That I *do* have a heart. This is critical, especially when they discover that *I*, like Chris Isaak, did a very bad thing.

Well, fuck Tarantino, and the Coens, and M. Night. And Kubrick, and Spielberg, and Coppola for that matter. No one—except film freaks like me—even cares who they are anyway. This is *my* show. Here goes.

Opening scene: Take one.

DEZ

Jonah shoots me a warning glare when the girls leave to go to the bathroom, which, by the way, is really annoying. I'll never understand the whole pissing-in-a-pair thing. I ignore him and pick at the heaping pile of wilted nachos—a waste of my favorite food court meal, but I've lost my appetite.

Spending a Saturday night on a double date at the Heights Mall is about as pitiful as it gets. The once-happening place has become a no man's land. Over the past few years, almost half of the stores have gone out of business. Even the food court options have been whittled down to Big Burgers, Taco Bell, and a small snack shop. You can almost see the tumbleweeds blowing by.

If this were a movie, we'd be at a homecoming dance or a football game or a romantic autumn hayride. But this year's homecoming was canceled, our football team sucks, and after a teacher was killed in our high school last month, the town is pretty much keeping to a nine p.m. curfew.

"Desmond," Jonah says, pulling away my plate of

processed cheese sauce. "If you don't stop being a complete douche, I'm going to kill you."

"Please do." I bang my head on the table and ignore his empty threats. "Put me out of my misery."

"That's great, Dez," he says on the verge of what I'd call a whine. "Real nice. I just needed you to be my wingman for one night, that's all I asked. Just one night. When have I ever asked you for anything?"

And here comes the guilt trip. I deserve it. Jonah has never really asked me for anything. No, he's more of a giver. Always been that way, even when we were kids.

FLASHBACK SEQUENCE
INT. ELECTRONICS STORE—DAY

A 10-year-old JONAH and DESMOND browse the racks of video games.

JONAH
You need to get this game, Dez.
I got it for my birthday and it's sweet.

DEZ
(rubs fingers together)
Can't. No dinero.

JONAH reaches in his pocket and pulls out a wad of crumpled bills.

JONAH
Well, I do. I have lots of dinero.

DEZ
No. No way. That's your birthday money.

JONAH
So? It's no fun to play Mario Brothers by yourself. You need it too. Then we can play against each other.

JONAH makes a goofy face at his friend, grabs the game, and heads to the check-out counter. DEZ chases after him…

END FLASHBACK

PRESENT DAY
INT. THE HEIGHTS MALL—EVENING
DEZ smiles at the memory.

Yeah, Jonah's always been that way.

Big surprise, I kept that game—and beat Jonah at it every time we played. The least I can do for the guy is help him look good in front of his date. But I just can't get into it.

"If you don't put that phone away, I swear to God," Jonah says.

"Yours is out."

"Yeah, but I haven't been glued to it all night like you have."

He's right, yet I can't exactly tell him what I've been doing on my phone and why I need it tonight. Instead, I keep my transgressions to myself. Trouble is, they're piling up like the unwanted bills Mom used to keep in the kitchen drawer—

notices that meant our lights or telephone would soon be shut off. I worry what will happen to me when I can no longer close the drawer on my sins. I have no choice but to keep them hidden.

Jonah would never understand anyway. He's one of the good guys.

Sorry sap. He's totally flipped over his date. She's from the other side of the river, a town about twenty minutes from here. She had to lie to her parents about coming out to the Heights. After all the shit that went down last month, our little town is not exactly the place you'd want to send your daughters.

It goes both ways. People from the Heights generally don't care for people on the east side of the river—where the suburbs tend to be bigger, wealthier, and closer to the Twin Cities. And though her town isn't what you'd call sophisticated by any means, it's definitely (as Mom would say) *highfalutin'* compared to the Heights.

Jonah met Ms. High Society at a youth group thing last weekend. Her name is Sage or Cinnamon or some spice. I can't remember. I'm supposed to keep the Spice Girl's friend, what's-her-face, company while Jonah makes his move. But I've totally neglected my duties. I'm such a dick.

My phone buzzes and I practically fall out of my seat. The call I've been waiting for. I motion for Jonah to give me a minute. He bites his nails, cursing the day I was born.

The screen on my phone reads: *All ready to go. Are you sure?*

Do it! I type back.

Then I hold my breath.

If I knew then what I know now, I never would've sent that text. I wouldn't have done a lot of things. Yeah, if my life were a movie, I'd go back and edit out all the bad stuff. Leave it all on the cutting room floor.

But I can't. And now I will have to pay.

Big time.

After several uncomfortable moments, Jonah clears his throat.

"Okay, my bad," I say before checking my phone one last time. "Gimme another shot." I'm a sucker for a guy in lust. Jonah's date *is* pretty cute, and just because I'm not getting any doesn't mean I should deny my friend the opportunity.

"Yeah?" Jonah says, looking hopeful.

"Yeah." I pat his shoulder.

"Thanks, man."

"Okay. First order of business: stop with the nails." I swat his hand "Chicks hate that shit. It's disgusting."

Jonah nods and pulls his fingers from his mouth. "Check. Anything else?"

"Yeah, take this." I hand him my tin of Altoids. "Probably not a good idea to load your burger with onions when you're trying to impress a girl."

"See, this is what I need." Jonah flashes his gummy grin and pops a few mints. "My wingman is back."

When the girls—Ginger and Nicole, thank you very much—return, I do a complete 180.

"So," I say to Jonah, gearing up to make it a big production. "Are you getting the band together this weekend?"

He raises an eyebrow.

"You're in a band?" Ginger squeaks.

"Guitar and lead singer," I say.

While it's true that Jonah can sing, he's terrible at guitar and there hasn't been a band since eighth grade. But I have to do something. He's sinking over there.

"I'd love to hear you play sometime." Ginger laughs and whispers something to Nicole.

Jonah mouths *thank you* when she's not looking.

My work here is done.

Jonah and Ginger are deep in conversation the rest of the night and I work my hardest to keep Nicole entertained.

"So, Desmond Brandt, do you have a girlfriend?" she asks while twirling a clump of hair. I'm not sure if she's trying to be cute or sexy or what. But it's none of the above.

"Ah . . . not exactly," I say.

"Well . . . " She untangles her hand from the hair clump and rests it on the table, dangerously close to mine. "What *is* your status then? Exactly?"

"Long story. Let's just say it's complicated. You?" I ask, not caring to know the answer.

The next several minutes are a blur of Nicole telling me about all the guys who want her and why. I nod, smile, and do everything in my power to get through the night.

In the end, it's not too bad. I buy everyone churros, Jonah gets another date with Ginger, and there under the fluorescent lights of the food court, I become one of the best wingmen who has ever lived.

All is right with the world.

Until Monday.

RILEY

I free my hair from the braids Mom put in this morning and fan the long locks around my face to create a barrier between *me* and *them*. By fourth period the gossip has traveled far and wide. I try to ignore the stares and snickers as we walk down the hall. Libby, on the other hand, cannot. She flips people off, hurls insults, and is basically a nightmare our entire walk to the gym. What can I say? She always has my back.

I keep my head up, ears closed, and try not to look at my classmates' faces. This is how it goes around here. One wrong move, one bad rumor, one mistake, and it's social death row.

I'm the latest to be sentenced.

Move out of the way, everyone.

Dead girl walking.

We pass the lockers and classrooms without saying a word. The school's walls and floor are beginning to show their age—they're grungy and tired with wrinkles and cracks, peeling paint and water damage. Poor old thing; it's only going to get worse until our district can afford a face-lift. And *that* will come long after I graduate this spring.

In the Heights, a deteriorating high school is the least of our worries. Most people are just trying to make it, and many are hanging on by their fingernails. In an area plagued by unemployment, things like housing foreclosures, car repos, and bankruptcy are as common as grocery shopping, football practice, and church on Sunday.

And that's only the half of it.

So far, my family's been lucky. Dad is tenured at the community college and Mom works at a Montessori daycare, which is pretty much foolproof—bad economy or not, people need a place to put their kids. Libby's family hasn't been as fortunate. Her dad lost his job a few months ago. Things must be getting tight at home because she's always "forgetting" her lunch money, and more often than not, she's "just not that hungry." Not to mention she took on a job doing janitorial work at the Java House and she hates to clean. But she makes minimum wage and gets all the free coffee she can drink, so she's not complaining.

"Are you sure you're up for this?" Libby looks up at me when we get to the locker room.

"Does it matter? I have to face her sooner or later."

I'd rather it be later.

Libby and I go to our lockers and pull out our standard-issue gym uniforms: navy shorts and white T-shirts. Tori and Natalie are just steps behind us. At the end of our row, they begin to change out of their designer clothes. Of course they wouldn't be caught dead wearing anything from our ghetto mall or Target, so they go into the city for two-hundred-dollar jeans, trendy flats, and modest skirts that hang below their fingertips. Personally, I like Target and even a few shops at the mall. But who are we kidding? I have no one to impress.

Tori looks down our row and shudders. "Let's get away from the dykes," she says to Natalie. "I wouldn't want to turn them on before class."

And so it begins.

Tori Devlin is the head of the Christian brigade. She wears a purity ring and leads a group of dedicated wannabes we call the Tori Rollers. Tori's dad is the mayor of our little rundown city and is currently running for a second term, so Tori's been helping him preach family values and morality out on the campaign trail. Here at school, that means hating on anyone or anything deemed unchristianlike.

Now that the cat's out of the bag, that means *me*.

"Keep dreaming," Libby yells as Tori and Natalie retreat to the other row of lockers.

"Nice comeback," I scoff.

Libby shrugs. "You know I'm not great under pressure."

That is so not true. If there is one person you want to have by your side in a disaster-type situation, it's Libby. In kindergarten, she helped me take care of my bloody nose after the boys bombarded me in the face with the four-square ball. Then she kicked the ball over the playground fence so they couldn't play with it anymore. We've been friends ever since. Libby knows how to handle the sticky situations and she's more loyal than a golden retriever. She is also—unfortunately—a little hotheaded.

I sigh and stretch my neck. It's going to be a long hour.

"What?" Libby throws her arms up at me before pulling on her tee.

"Do you have to antagonize them?" I ask.

Libby's head pops through her shirt and now that she's looking directly at me, I can see the dark bags that hang under her eyes. "They're the ones calling us names."

"I know." I bump her hip. "And, you are so *not* a dyke."

She makes a pouty face. "No shit. Guilt by association."

Poor Libby has been guilty by association since Saturday night, after my very public outing.

We change and walk into the gym. It's full of ratty volleyball nets and bodies and smells like mold and sweat. The boys are bunched up in one group at the end of the room and the girls huddle in another cluster. Coach Keller stands in the middle with his clipboard, ready to choose the team captains.

I spot Emma against the gym wall and ache instantly. The pain starts in my stomach, moves to my chest and up my neck, and finds a resting place behind my left temple. Emma doesn't notice. Her head is down as she twists the ring on her finger.

Up until Saturday, Emma and I were a couple. Maybe that's too strong a word. We were dating. Secretly. I didn't want it to be that way but the Heights is not exactly the place for non-traditional lifestyles. Last week, Tori and her friends came to school one morning wearing T-shirts for the Day of the Righteous. Apparently it's some religious movement to help gay people become straight. It's the second year they've done it, but this year, Mayor Devlin had the whole congregation from his church saying prayers outside the school—and then his daughter went around the halls telling everyone she suspected of being gay that they were going to hell for their sins.

Most people don't even understand what the Day of the Righteous is all about. But that doesn't stop them from pumping their fists, saying "Righteous, Dude," all day long. And that includes some of the teachers.

Though Emma and I were both technically in the closet, rumors have been circulating about me for years. *Is she? Isn't she?* The problem was, even *I* wasn't sure.

Now it doesn't matter if I am or not. Emma decided to out me at the Java House over the weekend. Emma works at the Java House too, and I'd always meet up with her after her shift. Saturday night was no different than any other, until this happened.

So . . . everyone knows.

Looking back, the whole thing seems like it was staged. I could almost hear a director's voice in my ears . . .

Riley and Emma breakup scene.

And ... Action!

"Riley, not everyone is gay," Emma yells, in front of the whole crowd, after I make my way to our booth.

"I think you're nice and all," she continues. "But I'm not into you that way. Please just back off."

Everyone bursts out in laughter—at least it seems like everyone. I stand there in shock, like a bucket of cold water has been dumped on my head. I'm shivering, watching people in slow motion. Emma's face is frozen, not giving anything away.

Then Libby sweeps in, leads me away by my arm, and tells the pack of onlookers exactly what they can do with their body parts. Thankfully, Java management isn't around, because I'm pretty sure telling patrons to go fuck themselves would be cause for termination.

Here in the gym, Libby lifts her chin in my direction—her way of telling me to be strong. She knows I've been sick all day, worrying about seeing Emma again. Emma's been MIA since it happened. I've tried to get ahold of her but I've had no luck. There've been no texts, no email, no messenger pigeons. Nada. I haven't seen her in any of our school meeting spots either.

She's at the other end of the gym and I want to go to her, but there's no way we can talk here—in front of everyone. She's made that perfectly clear.

One month ago, it was the two of us having fun in this very room. Totally G-rated, but it felt like the beginning of something. Then we started meeting up for lunch, spending time at the coffee shop drinking mochas, and hiding in the bookshelves at the library sharing secrets. We talked about my plans to go to acting school.

I already have applications in at my top choices: Tisch School of the Arts at NYU, Northwestern, and the Guthrie program at the University of Minnesota. I want to be invited to the first round of artistic reviews and auditions, and that means starting early. If all of these fall through, it's community college for me. *With my dad.* If it actually comes to that, I hope to be struck by lightning and live the rest of my days at Good Samaritan's Home for Vegetables.

Emma, conversely, wanted to stick around the Heights once she became a vet. Her family lives in town but has some land in the country where they have a few horses and chickens. Emma would live out there if she could. She hopes to take it over one day, though I can't fathom why she'd want to stay around here—a place where she has to hide.

Now I won't get to know that hidden piece of her. Yet, with all that's happened, I feel like it's a piece of *me* that's missing. A piece I hadn't even realized I'd found.

"Move in, folks," Coach K shouts, crammed between his chosen captains—Tori and one of the jock girls. The chosen guys stand to the left.

Great, it's time for the obligatory picking of the teams.

Emma stands up to join the group. Her sandy hair is pinned back, but a loose curl has escaped and falls across her face. I fight the urge to brush it away. When I look closer, I see that something has shifted; her expression is different. All the warmth is gone from her face. She's a stranger, and I can feel the barricade between us. I wish I could break through to get to my friend.

"Look at Coach K, loving life." Marcus chuckles. "You could put *me* in that hottie sandwich any time."

Marcus is what you'd call the rebound guy. You know

the type—the kind of guy who preys on the newly single and depressed. Every high school has a Marcus. Once a girl's relationship status turns to *it's complicated*, he begins the hunt. When Paige Han's boyfriend was killed in a motorcycle accident sophomore year, Marcus only waited a few days to strike. For some gross reason, it works. He dated Paige for six months.

These days, Paige avoids him like an STD. Tori, on the other hand, doesn't seem to notice his indiscretions. Their families run in the same crowd, so they're pretty tight.

Each captain calls out names. The jock guys are all selected first—big surprise—and then there's a bunch of high-fiving and ass-slapping. I feel like I'm going to choke on all the testosterone.

Soon the only guys left are the small, shy, and uncoordinated. Those unfortunate souls are bypassed altogether as the Tori Rollers and the jock girls are picked.

Then Tori takes inventory of her choices. "Gosh, who should we choose next?" she asks her team, fluttering her fingers across her lips. "The dorks or the dykes?"

Tori's friends giggle in unison and Marcus gives her a fist bump.

Coach K gets in on it too. He smirks and turns his head, pretending not to hear. He's notorious for his selective listening. Last year, he stood by while two senior guys tormented a freshman during weight training. The seniors were supposed to be spotting the kid during his bench presses but, instead, they let the bar drop on the boy's chest and left him to struggle under the weight. It was to toughen him up, they said. I guess the kid fractured his clavicle. Coach got some grief from a few parents and teachers for his negligence, but nothing ever seems to stick to that guy.

Jonah looks over at me and gives me his puppy dog eyes, but he doesn't say a word about Tori's comments. They go to the same church and Jonah would never cross her.

"Just pick the teams, Tori—we can do without your commentary," Stella pipes up. Stella's a loner who transferred here last year. I used to feel sorry for her but I think maybe she's onto something, steering clear of these idiots.

"Yeah, just hurry up," another guy yells from the crowd.

At least I have a few allies left.

Circles of teams begin to form while the rest of us losers lean up against the wall, wondering how long this torture can continue. I settle in because I don't have a chance of getting picked until the very end. Not with Tori running the show.

Libby shuffles her feet, unable to stand still.

By the end, we're the only two remaining. I'm okay with it, but there's no reason why Libby still hasn't been picked. She's an awesome athlete and, at six feet tall, she stands almost a foot above my measly five-two frame. When we're together, I look like her sponsored child from the Big Brothers/Big Sisters program.

Tori sighs before making her last choice, looking us both up and down. "Okay, we'll take Libby."

And then there was one.

Jock Girl doesn't even say my name. It's simply implied that I'm left for her team. She turns around toward the net and the team follows. It's almost comical. Maybe. If it was happening to someone else.

The four teams take their place on the court. My team is up against Tori's.

Perfect.

Once we finally start to play, Libby gets her revenge. Within seconds of the whistle, she spikes the ball. But instead of crossing the net, it comes down on Tori.

Hard.

Libby shrugs like it's an accident.

Then she gets serious and pretty much smokes everyone on our side of the net. The girl is on fire. Her own team has a hard time *not* cheering.

On my team, however, they shut me out.

I don't care. I just hover in position and try not to watch as Marcus eyes Emma, ready to catch her on the rebound.

God, I hate this place.

DEZ

EXT. THE FROSTS' FRONT PORCH—
NIGHT

The camera moves in tight on RILEY FROST, a beautiful 17-year-old girl with long dark hair. She sits on the porch tucked into a ball. Her arms hug her knees tight.

CUT TO:

CLOSE UP: RILEY
She looks up and her face is red and blotchy. She's been crying.

I do this a lot—watch my life from the eyes of a director. It's like I'm watching a movie. Sometimes it's easier to deal with than the real thing. It doesn't hurt as much or something. Or maybe I've just completely lost it. I've heard that's what happens when you spend too much time behind the camera. There's a ton of weird stories about the great filmmakers.

Take Stanley Kubrick. I guess he used to shoot at visitors on his front lawn when he wanted to be alone. Then there's Werner Herzog, who's known for all kinds of crazy. He once cooked and ate his shoe in public after losing a bet. And look at Woody Allen. He married his girlfriend's twenty-year-old daughter when he was, like, sixty.

So maybe I'm not that bad.

My headlights catch Riley on her front porch as I pull into the driveway, and my face is burning. Riley left school early and missed rehearsal tonight, so I haven't seen her since this morning.

Our families have lived next door to each other since before we were born. Our moms became best friends after Joan and Ken adopted Riley from Russia. We were both almost two years old and became instant playmates. Our parents always joked that we'd get married someday. I thought they might be right—until I found out about Rye.

She stays frozen in a ball and doesn't notice me as I pull up, or when I slam the car door, or when I cross my yard to get to hers. She doesn't see me until I'm practically on top of her.

"Hey." I nudge my New Balance into her Pumas.

She coughs and blinks real hard—and just like that, the anguish covering her face is wiped clean, replaced with a smile and bright eyes.

"Hey to you." Her Puma nudges back.

I'm not in Riley's gym class, but Jonah's given me the play-by-play of Tori's abuse. It's been beyond rough.

"We missed you tonight." I grab a seat next to her on the

porch. The paint is flaking off the wood floor and Riley mindlessly picks at it. I was supposed to paint it for them over the summer, but Joan and Ken decided to wait one more year. They've been saying "one more year" since we graduated from junior high.

The heat from our Indian summer has finally broken and a cool breeze is now coming through. Autumn is here. The porch light shines on Riley's bare arms, little scrawny things sporting goose bumps.

"I'm sorry about rehearsal, Dez," she says. For a second, I can see what looks to be a flash of regret. "I just wasn't up for it."

I unzip my hoodie and wrap it around her shoulders.

She snuggles into the sweatshirt and rests her head on my arm. It's something she's done so many times. Still, I have to steady myself when she's this close, so I play the game *What's NOT hot*. I flip through images in my head. What's not hot?

My mom.

Jonah.

That documentary about how fast food is made.

Riley takes a breath and looks at me. I can see the sadness in her eyes. She's exposed and vulnerable. My gaze travels down her face to her lips and…

Puppies, not hot.

Grandma Brandt, so not hot.

Snowstorm. Cold. Cold. Cold.

I get my thoughts—and crotch—under control and listen as she goes on.

"It's bad, Dez. And not only for me. I'm taking Libby down too. That's the last thing she needs right now."

"Oh, come on," I say, feeling my stomach churn. "It can't be that bad."

Can it?

In my head, I see Riley and Libby on an execution platform like in that old Clint Eastwood movie *Hang 'Em High.* I used to watch all the old westerns with my Grandpa. In this one, a bunch of guys are sentenced to death by hanging so the "authority" decides to execute them all at the same time. The camera pans across the men as they stand on the platform, nooses around their necks, while the townspeople gather around salivating for blood. A preacher condemns them for their sins and the crowd breaks out in Bible hymns. Then the lawmen turn a lever and the next thing you see are the men's dangling feet.

I squeeze my eyes shut and shake away the image.

"Oh, it's that bad," Riley says. "Didn't you know? Now that I've scared Emma off, Libby's become my new lezzy lover. Everyone's talking about it."

"Don't worry, it's just the drama of the moment. It'll all blow over." I hope.

"I don't know. Things are so effed up."

It's true, things *are* fucked up around here—just like the Wild West. It all started when Tori's dad, Mayor Devlin, kicked off his campaign for re-election last spring. During his first term, he was investigated for hiring his friends to city jobs and cashing in on political favors. It was a huge story—the Minneapolis media even covered it. He was never charged with anything, though, and he's been on a mission to clear his good name ever since.

This year, his campaign has focused on ethics, morals, and family values. He's been all over town talking about saving *this* and protecting *that*. Before all this Devlin business, I don't remember things being such a big deal. I don't know, it seemed like people just kept their opinions to themselves. But now everything is up for debate. You can feel the tension in the air.

And that's not the worst of it. Last month, Ms. Dunn—our humanities teacher and one of the people who started the Devlin investigation—was stabbed to death at school. She was Riley's favorite teacher, so Rye's had a double dose of shit to deal with.

Nobody really knows how the murder went down, and I... well, I have more details than I should. Details I've tried to erase from my memory. Images that creep into my dreams.

The official word is that Ms. Dunn was killed in the supply room at the end of the day. The janitor found her on his evening rounds. School had been in session less than a week. The newly sharpened pencils hadn't even had a chance to dull yet. It was a stranger who did it, they say. A random criminal looking for money or shelter or something to steal. They say it was quick and Ms. Dunn probably didn't even know what hit her.

They lie.

Technically, the investigation is still going on but without a murder weapon or a suspect, it's slow going. Of course, I got a peek at my stepfather's report and a look at the crime scene, so I have a bit more information than the average resident in the Heights.

A bunch of the morons at school are convinced it was Carl the Janitor. Poor old guy. There's no way he had the strength to kill Ms. Dunn in that way, but that didn't stop the assholes from tormenting him until he quit last week.

Yeah, between the Ms. Dunn murder mystery and the Devlin campaign, the local mob has been out with their torches. It's basically a free-for-all at school, and with Tori and her family at the helm, the teachers are too afraid to do anything about it. Nobody wants to risk their job or their funding… or their life for that matter. Everyone is scared.

That's why I'm *glad* Riley and Emma broke up. There, I said it. Things will be much better for Rye now, even if she doesn't see it yet.

I squeeze her a little closer. "I'm sorry, babe. Are you okay?"

"C'est la vie." Riley flips her wrist.

"Yeah, but it still sucks."

"I don't know. I just don't get it." She sighs. "Only a few people knew about me and Emma—really only you, Jonah, and Libby. Not like you guys would say anything. Why did she make that scene? If she didn't want to be with me, why couldn't she dump me in private?"

"I don't know, Rye." My stomach clenches. "Maybe she got scared."

She goes still, holding everything inside. We sit there like that for a while, Riley under the shield of my arm but still so far away.

"Hey, what about you? How was the double date?" She tries to change the subject.

"Not bad," I say. "I made a young man very happy. I am Wingman," I say, striking my best superhero pose.

"Oh yeah?" She laughs.

There's the sound I was waiting for. The sound I needed to hear.

"I was afraid Jonah's girl would drop him for you at first sight," she adds. "Not a smart move choosing Mr. Tall, Dark, and Delicious as your wingman."

"Guys don't think about shit like that," I say. "Why? Is that how you see me—tall, dark, and delicious?" I pull her closer and give her my best smoldering look.

"That's how everyone sees you." She punches my arm and breaks my hold on her, reminding me that this flirtation is completely futile. "Well, D." She stands up, signaling that it's time to go. "It's a school night."

"Okay, Mom." I take her hint.

"See you in the a.m."

I give her a two-finger salute.

"Good night, Dez."

"'Night."

I head across the lawn, home to my mom and my stepdad, Bernie. They're curled up on the couch watching Letterman. Or, to be more accurate, they're going at it in front of Letterman.

God, my eyes. My eyes!

"Hi there, buddy." Bernie sits up quickly, looking like

he just got busted with weed or something. "How was your night?"

"Good, good." I stare at the TV, trying not to make eye contact. "I'm beat though, going up."

"Okay, sweetheart," Mom says, smoothing down her hair. "See you in the morning."

I try to shake away the disturbing image and make a beeline for my room.

Actually, I have to say, Bernie is cool as shit. I was relieved when he and Mom got together—especially after years of all the tools sniffing around her. And since Bernie is a cop, I feel like I can finally let my guard down at home.

Inside my sanctuary, the curtains flap in the breeze from the open window. I see Riley in the gap between them. Just as I thought, she hasn't gone inside. She's still sitting on her porch, her shoulders all hunched over. She starts to shake.

I turn away because it gives me physical pain to see her like this. To know it's my fault. I know I've got to stop. I'm just not sure I know how.

I close my window and try *not* to think of Riley outside.

Instead, I grab one of my many video cameras. My room is a shrine to cinema. I have vintage film reels and old studio lights scattered around. The walls are covered in hundreds of movie tickets and posters of my favorites, like *Reservoir Dogs*, *Fight Club*, and *The Godfather*. Mr. Pink, the *Fight Club* dudes, and Don Corleone are all staring at me now. They shake their heads in disgust and tell me I'm whipped over a girl I'll never have.

I ignore them and go to work on the film—the piece we'll

be submitting to the festival next month, the piece that could get me into the film program at Columbia. In the viewfinder, images move across the tiny screen, but nothing registers in my head.

Riley's still out there.

I put down the camera and grab my notebook. I start to outline the scenes we need to shoot tomorrow, but soon my outline turns to doodles and chicken scratch.

She's still out there.

I sit on my bed and put my ear buds in, closing my eyes as the music fills my head. The Kings of Leon do nothing to take my mind off Rye.

The Godfather tells me to make her an offer she can't refuse.

I tell him to shut his mafia-ass up.

I go to turn off the light. It reminds me of the game Riley and I played when we were kids. Rye used to be deathly afraid of the dark, but she was too embarrassed to tell her parents. Even then, she tried to be tough. I, in my infinite ten-year-old wisdom, came up with a plan to help. I told her that she could signal me with her lights when she couldn't sleep. And when she did, I'd go to my window and stand guard—watch her room—to be sure nothing happened.

Rye would flick her lights when she needed me. Slow, fast, fast, fast. Slow. It was our version of Morse code.

I would answer back with three quick flicks of my light switch. Then I'd go to my window. She'd look out of hers and wave, and finally drift off to sleep knowing everything was safe.

It took her about a month to get over her fears. For me, that meant a month of standing guard at the window and falling asleep in class after my late nights. It was worth every second.

I flick my lights now, seven years later, and go to the window. Riley looks up. She smiles and waves.

After a few minutes she goes inside.

And answers me with her lights.

RILEY

The next morning, as I get ready for another day on social death row, I'm welcomed by a breakfast that I would definitely choose to be my last meal—banana chocolate chip pancakes. It's quite a step up from the normal knock-off cereal I've become accustomed to. I mean, the Fruit Rings, Happy Shapes, and Crispy Rice taste okay, but breakfast is not the same without the toucan and the leprechaun and Snap, Crackle, and Pop. It's lame, but I really miss those guys.

Dad looks at me over his glasses and smiles. He quickly plants a kiss on my forehead and gets back to the stove. Instead of his usual morning routine of grading English Lit papers for his class, he's cooking. And instead of rushing around getting ready for her day rounding up toddlers, Mom sits at the table with two monster cups of steaming coffee.

Yep, they know something's up.

I sit next to Mom and she quickly turns over the newspaper. It's too late. I've already caught the headline: *Community Honors Slain Teacher*. As if the newspaper will suddenly remind me that Ms. Dunn was murdered. As if I don't think about her every day. She wasn't just my teacher; she was so much more.

Mom pushes the paper to the side and hands me the coffee cup. I soak in the caffeine and it helps clear my head.

Mom gives me a few minutes before she dives in.

"So, do you want to talk about what's been going on the past few days?"

"Not particularly," I tell her.

"Riley, you've been so quiet and not eating. I'm starting to get worried." She leans in and holds my hand. "Talk to me—maybe I can help."

I shake her off and take a gulp of coffee.

"It's nothing I can't handle."

"But, honey—"

"It's okay." I cut her off. My parents don't know about Emma and I'm not about to play catch-up. Not that they wouldn't understand—they're pretty open about that kind of thing. Dad even has a few gay friends from the college. But I wasn't about to come out to my parents before I was absolutely sure.

And Emma made me promise to keep *us* a secret. I did, because I wanted to keep her happy and I liked having her all to myself. I liked that I didn't have to share that part of my life with anyone. I did at first, anyway. It was exciting. The soft looks that passed between us at school; the love notes she left in my locker; the way we held hands in her car when we snuck out for lunch. It was the first time I felt like someone could actually see *me*. The real me.

It's hard to breathe just thinking about it.

"I'll tell you everything, Mom," I assure her. "Just not now, okay?"

From the corner of my eye I can see Dad motioning to Mom. He's pushing his hands down—the universal sign for *take it easy.*

I offer up a silent thank you for giving me a dad who understands.

"Okay, Riley." Mom sighs. "You'll come to me when you're ready?" We both know it's not a question. It's an order.

"I will," I reply, happy to say anything that will get her off my back. For the rest of breakfast, we play a normal family—we make small talk, eat banana chocolate chip pancakes, and pretend nothing's wrong.

At school, Dez and I spend first period hanging in the edit suite going over footage from one of my scenes. It's a tiny, soundproof room. Three of the walls are covered with gray acoustic foam and the back wall is glass with a small sliding door. A computer used for digital editing, an old monitor, a table, and two rolling chairs take up the entire space.

We're working on a short feature for the Midwest High School Film Festival, one of the most important events around here for film. Our school is hosting it this year, and a lot of the local colleges will be coming to hold interviews and auditions. This could put me and Dez on the map. Plus, the scholarship opportunity is huge.

This is the project that's going to get both of us out of the Heights.

Alternate Realities is Dez's baby. It's a dark story about a strange girl who is the pariah of the school. She's odd, awkward, and alone. So when she's given the chance to enter an alternate reality where she's beautiful, popular, and revered, she doesn't think twice. Dez calls it the female version of *Fight Club*.

It's really pretty brilliant.

We go through my scenes, starting with the footage we shot last month. Dez fast-forwards to a medium shot of me and Jonah in a classroom. Ms. Dunn's classroom. She let us use her room to film that day. Her last day.

For obvious reasons, we haven't gone through this footage yet—but we no longer have an option. We're getting close to crunch time. My stomach turns as I remember that day, but I power through it and concentrate on Dez.

"Okay, this scene here." Dez freezes the video and goes into director mode. It helps me focus. "This is what I'm talking about. See how scared you look?"

"Yeah." I watch my face on the computer screen. I really do look completely terrified.

"I want more of this in the beginning." Dez taps his finger on my video face. "Rye, your character has been picked on, snubbed, and abused for years. Going to school for her is like going to war. Every. Single. Day. Imagine what that would be like."

I laugh. Of course I can imagine what that's like. I'm living it right now.

It sucks.

"Shit, Rye." Dez drops his head. "I'm sorry. I didn't mean—"

He looks up and wraps an arm around me, and I close my eyes for a second. Dez is one of those people who just draws you in. Even before the latest dumping, Dez was always telling me I'm too good for the idiots at our school. Too smart, self-aware, original.

I have to laugh, because he must think the same of himself since he's never dated anyone in the Heights. And he could. Any girl at school would be thrilled to have him.

"It's okay," I say, leaning into him. "Sometimes life imitates art, right?" I add, all drama geeky.

"Rye, believe me, you are *not* anything like this character." He grabs the script and starts flipping through the pages. "Hey, if it's too hard to play this part right now, I could do a rewrite. I still have time."

"Um, no—you don't. Plus, this is your masterpiece. Don't worry, I'll channel my pain." I give him a quick wink. "Come on, let's finish going through it."

Dez hits play and we watch the scene. He continues to give direction, but I can tell he's taking it easy on me.

I think about what he said: *your character has been picked on and abused for years.* I think about all the insults Tori has spewed at me. The jokes I've had to brush off. My horrible track record in relationships. Ever since I started high school, I've been dumped by both boys and girls—I've become an equal opportunity dumpee. And that's all before things even get going. I'm a senior and I haven't even made it to second base yet.

So, playing the part of a social pariah? Yes, this might just be the easiest role I've ever had.

Dez's phone rings. It's the theme to *The Godfather*. He picks it up and looks at the caller ID.

"Shit, it's Jonah. This might take a minute."

Dez motions for me to keep working while he heads out of the edit suite. I continue to watch myself—something I detest. I jot down a few notes until the scene is over. But once my face leaves the screen, the video keeps going. Looks like Dez forgot to turn it off during our break.

I remember how we left to get snacks out of the vending machine that afternoon. Dez bought a Snickers. Jonah chose a bag of chips. I got M&Ms. Of course I remember that day perfectly—I had to tell the cops about it over a dozen times because we were the last known people in Ms. Dunn's classroom. She had a staff meeting that day, so we had the room to ourselves.

I'm about to fast-forward the video when I hear a voice.

"Hurry up, they'll be back any minute," the voice says through the speakers. I recognize it immediately. It belongs to Libby.

She walks into the frame and my scalp tingles.

What is she doing there? On our video?

I don't think I want to see this. I don't want to know this.

"Where did that bitch put it?" asks a different voice. A guy's voice. It's weirdly distorted. I stare at the empty screen while the conversation continues.

"In the desk," Libby says.

"Find it. That shit can be linked back to me. I ordered it online."

"Shut up and keep a lookout."

I can hear the guy's voice though he never enters the screen. The desk drawers open and close and there's a rumbling of papers.

"If Dunn fucks me up because of this ... " the guy says.

"She doesn't even know it's yours," Libby says. "I'm the one on the line here."

"Fuck, they're coming," the guy says.

Libby's body runs past the screen. And then they're gone.

My heart races and I can't begin to process what I've just watched. Instinctively, I hit *stop*. I need to know more, but I don't want anyone else to see it. I need a copy.

I don't have much time. I snag a DVD from the stack on the table. I shove it into the computer, convert the file to DVD, and click the *start burning* button.

I hear someone's feet shuffle outside the door. The video is recording and I can't stop it, so I stand up to block the monitor.

Just in time.

There's a tap on the sliding glass door. Marcus smiles and peeks his head in. "Watching your girl-on-girl porn in here?"

I turn my head but keep my body angled, strategically covering the monitor. "What do you want, Marcus?"

"Just replacing the bulbs on these babies." He signals to the lights. Marcus' dad owns the only photo studio in town, and that means Marcus has complete access to all the lighting gear, backdrops, and props he can get his creepy little hands on. With our non-existent budget, Dez really had no choice but to let him join the crew. Strangely, he's also a hard worker. So I put up with him, even if I hear "giggity" in my head after every one of his sentences.

"Well, don't let me stop you," I tell him.

"Okay, okay." Marcus smirks. "I just thought you might be watching something interesting in here, that's all."

"Whatever." I try to wrap it up, sure that Dez is on his way back. "Anything else? I'm trying to work."

"Work? Oh ... that's what you call it?" He grins.

"Goodbye, Marcus."

He shuffles away and I get back to the video. It's almost done recording. Then I hear Dez's voice; he's still on the phone.

Come on, come on, come on.

The monitor finally goes black and the computer ejects the DVD. I stuff it into my bag, close the video file, and hit *delete* so it doesn't end up in the wrong hands. I can't risk Dez going back to look at it. I finish just as he says "later" into the phone.

"Sorry, Rye." He pops his head in. "I've wasted all our time. Should we finish this after rehearsal?"

"No," I say, a little too fast.

"Oh. Kay." Dez tips his head.

"I mean, I think we should just re-shoot that scene. I know I can do it better."

"Really?"

"Yes. Trust me."

"Yeah, okay. We'll reshoot."

"Great." I exhale. Guilt tears at me for lying to Dez, but I can't tell him about this. His stepdad's a cop, for God's sake. Plus, he doesn't even like Libby. Not after she tried to steal Reed—one of my many dumpers—out from under me sophomore year.

That's Dez's version of what happened, anyway. Libby swears it was Reed who came after her, but Dez isn't convinced. He calls her Slippery Libby behind her back. Not that creative, but it stuck.

Right now, I can't think about that. I don't even care anymore. The only thing I can do at this moment is protect Libby, at least until I know more.

Oh Libby, what did you get yourself into this time?

DEZ

“See you at the taping,” I tell Riley when I drop her at the door for second period, lingering a little longer than I should. I know she’s still upset over Emma, but there’s no way she’ll let me in.

It’s for the best. That’s what I have to remember.

Rye gives me an unconvincing smile. She is so strong and feisty, and yet soft and delicate at the same time. There’s always a battle going on inside her; I like watching to see which side will win. Her energy is magnetic and pulses out of her. It’s like a gravitational pull that holds me there in the doorway until Tori shows up.

“Excuse me, guys.” Tori moves between us and cuts the connection. “I need to put these up.” She gestures to the stack of flyers in her arms before handing one to each of us. Mayor Devlin has donated a memorial plaque for Ms. Dunn, and they’re holding the dedication in the school garden next week.

That’s guilt for ya. Sure, the Devlins may have played

nice with Ms. Dunn after the investigation, but it was no secret they hated her guts.

"Yeah, nice PR stunt," Riley says as she reads the flyer.

I couldn't have said it better myself.

"It's called being a good Christian, Riley."

"Whatever." Riley snorts. She says goodbye to me with her eyes and turns into the room.

"Hope to see you there," Tori yells to Riley's back. Then she winks at me and clicks off.

I stay in the doorway just long enough to catch Riley as she turns around, her silky hair swinging across her shoulders as she walks to her desk. Then her shirt rises up and for a second I see a sliver of her back—the part that curves right above her ass—before she pulls the shirt down.

I can't get the image out of my head as I make my way to Trig.

"Dez!" a girl's voice echoes in the hallway, forcing the picture of Riley to dissolve.

Emma moves toward me, and though my first thought is to keep walking, I wait for her to catch up. She's in my next class so there's no escaping her. When she gets up close, I can't make eye contact. She looks terrible. Her eyes are bloodshot and her skin is covered in red blotches. It makes me itchy.

"How's Riley holding up?" she whispers.

Here we go.

"Why are you asking me? I haven't been in gym with you guys while Tori's been chewing her a new one every day."

Emma winces. "You know I never wanted this to happen."

"Right," I spit, wanting to blame someone, anyone, other than myself.

"Don't you dare blame *me* for this." Emma's lips quiver.

Can't you see that I have no choice?

"It doesn't really matter," I tell her, not wanting to engage any more than I have to. "What do you want, Emma?" I ask. My voice softens; I'm worried that she might break.

She reaches into her bag and pulls out a note from the inside of a book. "Could you give her this?"

"What is it?" I meet her eyes.

"A note," she stutters. "To explain a little. Don't worry, it's not the whole story. But I want... I need... Riley to understand that I really do care about her."

I say nothing.

"You can read it if you don't trust me."

More silence.

"Dez, please."

I hold out my hand and nod.

It couldn't hurt to give it to Rye. It might even make things easier for her, stop her from second-guessing herself all the time. Make her realize this wasn't *her* fault.

My hand clenches the paper and I shove it in my pocket. I'll give it to her after rehearsal. Emma gives me a sad smile, and I return it.

It was the right thing to do.

Done.

But in class, I feel the note burning a hole inside my pocket. I stare out the window at the empty football field behind the school, with its chipped goalposts and faded hash marks on the turf.

My mind drifts.

In my daydreams, I see myself giving the note to Riley. She reads it, sighs, and falls in my arms. *Closure.*

The next second, I'm dropped into another scene. In this one, Rye falls back into *Emma's* arms. *Reconciliation.*

Fast-forward. Rewind. Fast-forward. Rewind.

The scenes play in my head all through class.

After the bell rings and I'm out of Emma's watchful gaze, a different scene plays out in front of me. This time, I find a quiet space, shred the piece of paper, and throw it in the trash.

This scene is real. I blink into the present and feel the paper in my hands as I destroy the evidence in Ms. Dunn's empty classroom. Like Tyler Durden says in *Fight Club*, "You wanna make an omelette, you gotta break some eggs." I feel sick just thinking about all eggs I'm going to have to break before all of this is done.

I slide into a desk and rest my head. I can't undo it now.

In the room, a poster of Shakespeare hangs on the wall, and statues and art rest on a shelf filled with books and CDs. Ms. Dunn has been gone a month but her room sits untouched. She didn't have family so nobody came for her stuff. It all sits here now, forgotten.

I can't help wonder if she's still here. Watching. What would she think about what happened? What would she think about me?

You're better than this, she'd always tell us when we messed up. Then she'd forgive and forget. Just as easy as that. She always saw the best in people. Rich, poor, jock, burner, Bible beater, goth. None of that mattered to her. Even with Devlin. After the investigation, he was relentless; but no matter how many times he came after her, petitioned her curriculum, or argued about policy, she never said a bad word about him.

This time, with everything that's happened, I'm not so sure she'd hold her tongue.

WHAT REALLY HAPPENED

INT. OLD HIGH SCHOOL SUPPLY ROOM FILLED WITH JUNK—EVENING

The camera moves in on MS. DUNN's face. RACHEL DUNN, high school humanities teacher, is a tall, thin woman in her early twenties. She has a pretty face and long auburn hair.

MS. DUNN rummages through boxes and crates. She gathers supplies for the school year, to supplement what she's already bought with her own money. She senses something behind her and turns around. Nobody's there.

MS. DUNN
(looks around the room and calls out)
Can I help you? Is anyone there?

A dark figure appears from the shadows. It could be a man or woman; we don't see the figure's face.

MS. DUNN CONT.
(exhales, relieved that she recognizes the person)
Oh, it's just you. You scared me for a minute. Why are you here? I thought I made myself perfectly clear in the classroom. I'm not changing my mind. It's over. Done.

There is a long period of silence. MS. DUNN fidgets but holds her ground. We see her clench her hands when they start to shake.

The dark figure storms off.

MS. DUNN turns around to face the table behind her. She braces her arms on the table and takes a few deep breaths before going back to her supplies. She laughs to herself and shakes her head.

CUT TO:

DARK FIGURE

The camera moves in on the dark figure's black shoes. The person walks through an empty hallway and slowly returns to the supply room. We see the figure stop at a shelf full of supplies. The person grabs something from the shelf with a gloved hand. We don't see what it is. The camera moves back to the black shoes. They keep walking.

RILEY

She follows me to my locker. I feel her on my heels. I put my hand to the combination and turn the knob: 20–4–32. My hand is sweaty, all the way down to my fingertips: 20–4–32. The numbers replay over and over in my head but I can't get to them fast enough.

She closes in.

The locker clicks and I push it open.

"Riley," she whispers on my neck. "I know what you saw. Now give me the DVD."

I reach into my locker and pull out the only weapon I can find. I turn to face her.

It's Libby, covered in blood.

"Riley." She rubs my shoulder. "Honey, wake up. You'll be late for school."

Light floods my room. I open my eyes. My lids are heavy and my vision is blurred, but I know I'm in my room. There's no locker, no Libby, no blood.

"Mom?" My voice is rough and my heart feels like it's going to jump out of my chest.

"Another bad dream?"

I nod.

"Do you need a personal day? I could stay with you and we could lie around in our PJs all day and watch movies."

It sounds perfect, but we both know she can't afford to take a day off.

"No, it's okay. It's just a stupid dream." *Or my subconscious telling me my best friend might be involved in a murder.*

Last night, I watched the video over and over again, trying to piece together what happened. The fact that Libby and this mystery guy were in Ms. Dunn's classroom the same day she was murdered is more than suspicious. I can't get it out of my head. Maybe this guy had it out for Ms. Dunn . . . maybe Libby knows what happened.

I never believed the police story—that it was a random act of violence—in the first place. I don't know. Maybe I've watched too many films, but I think Ms. Dunn had to know the killer. I've always has this eerie feeling that I can't explain. And now I feel like I owe it to her to follow this lead.

"Well, this might cheer you up," Mom says, holding out an opened envelope. "Sorry. I just had to look."

Once I see the Tisch logo on the envelope, I wake right up. Inside is an invitation. Mom hugs me. We knew it was coming, but now it's official—I'm going to New York in a few months for my artistic review.

Since I hardly slept last night, I'm running on fumes the rest of the day. At least the news of the Tisch invite creates a welcome distraction. I wave the invitation at Libby when she gets to my locker. I'm still reeling from what I saw in the editing suite yesterday, but I have to give her the benefit of the doubt—there has to be a perfectly logical reason for why she was in Ms. Dunn's classroom that day. I just need to find out what it was. I can't let my overactive imagination take over.

"Congratulations." Libby hugs me and I stiffen.

Just play it cool. Libby is your friend.

"It's nothing yet, just an invite to audition," I say.

"It's the beginning of good things, Rye. Plus, I hear New York girls are really hot."

Girls, right. "Well, I don't think that's even an option for me anymore. I'm done with all that."

"Done with all what?" she asks.

"Done with girls."

I've been thinking about it for a while. Even before Emma. I've been thinking about it since last year, back when I was crushing on Ms. Dunn and Dez busted me for it.

You're only going to get hurt, Rye, he said, after a few other choice words.

I didn't have to wait for that heartbreak, but then Emma came along and everything changed. I was exactly where I belonged and I thought everything would be okay. At least I was willing to take that chance.

Yeah, we saw how that worked out.

I guess Emma leaving me was the sign I needed to finally make the decision. I'm officially taking girls off the menu. It's a brilliant thought and makes perfect sense. I wonder why it took me so long.

Maybe Dez was right. Maybe "the gay thing" was all a phase.

Or maybe it's like that Kinsey scale. That tool to measure *how* gay or straight you are. Homer—what we call our film teacher because he eats a lot of donuts and looks like Homer Simpson—brought it up one day last year when we were giving our reviews of *Brokeback Mountain*. We spent the entire class arguing about whether or not the characters were straight, bi, or gay. This, of course, was before the Tori Rollers were running the school. When teachers like Ms. Dunn and Homer still had some power. Needless to say, *Brokeback Mountain* is no longer in the curriculum.

As we were all arguing, Homer tried to explain that most people are not totally gay or totally straight or even totally bi. And that your place on the Kinsey scale can change. It's super complicated, but I think that's what's happening to me. Maybe I'm moving closer to the *straight* end of the scale. Or... maybe I just want to.

"What, you're going for older women now?" Libby asks, completely clueless.

"No, I'm done with females." It feels good to say it, like I'm taking charge instead of handing over my heart to get stomped on over and over again.

"Come on. You're going to let a little breakup destroy you?"

"No, not destroy. I'm finally going to take control."

"So we're back to *boys* again, really?" she asks. "You're

giving me whiplash, Rye. You said you'd finally figured all this out."

I thought I had. I thought I'd finally realized where I belonged. Things felt so easy with Emma. Natural. And now I'm back to square one again. But after what I saw in the editing suite, none of this seems that important. A woman is dead. And her killer might be—in fact, probably is—still here.

I pray it has nothing to do with Libby.

Still, I can't help but think about Libby's rocky relationship with Ms. Dunn over the past year. I also can't help comparing every guy's voice I hear today to the voice on the video.

"Forget I said anything," I tell Libby. I had no idea she would get in such a huff. "Let's just keep this new development between us, 'kay?"

"Well, that's rich." She shakes her head.

"What?"

"You were so close to coming out, really coming out. But now that you're going back *in* the closet, you want to keep it a secret?"

"Why are you being so judgy?" I snap. "You're not perfect, ya know? I'm sure you have some secrets of your own."

That's an understatement—but now is not the time to ask.

"I'm not trying to be judgy, Riley, but…"

Libby stops because we smell her. You always smell her first, that sickly sweet and expensive designer perfume that fills the air wherever she goes.

Tori.

She swings around the corner, her usual peppy self. She's obviously heard everything.

"Telling secrets?" she asks.

"Like you haven't been eavesdropping," Libby says.

"I only heard the part about Riley's sex life." Tori laughs. "It must be really convenient to go back and forth, Riley. Dumped by a boy, no big deal, try a girl. Dumped by a girl, and now it's back to boys. Just face it—*everyone* thinks you're repulsive."

Libby tenses and I grab her arm to calm her.

Tori pats my back, turns on her heel, and bounces away down the hall.

The air suddenly warms at least twenty degrees. I exhale, realizing I'd been holding my breath.

"I wish you wouldn't take her shit," Libby says.

"What would you have me do?" Though I'd love to get in Tori's face and dish it right back, the truth is I'm scared. Anytime anyone messes with the Devlin family, something bad happens. Look at Ms. Dunn.

"I have an idea." Libby rubs her hands together. "I think it's time for some payback. How does Friday look for you?"

DEZ

INT. THE HALLWAY LEADING TO THE FILM CLASSROOM—AFTERNOON

Two guys, WILL THOMAS, short and slick high school drug dealer, and MARCUS FLYNN, handsome and built with ice blue eyes, huddle together a few doors from the film room. They talk in whispers but nothing is clear.

ZOOM IN:

CLOSE UP:
The boys' hands. They each conceal something as they make an exchange.

I hate the fact that I had no choice about Marcus joining the film crew. He's a total pig, but with his access to all of his dad's equipment and props, I couldn't say no. And today, here he is with the school's biggest freak. Like you can't tell he's buying shit. It's so obvious.

He must be getting his weekend stash.

It's finally Friday, and my patience is running thin. It's been a hellish week watching Rye suffer—especially with Tori on her case. I'm hoping today's filming will help take her mind off everything.

I walk up to Marcus and glare. "Dude, you know that shit is not allowed during production."

Marcus laughs. "Is the old man at home wearing off on you, Desmond?"

"Don't know what you're talking about, man." Will holds up his hands and slithers away.

"Look, I don't care what you do on your own time," I say. "But if you want to be on the crew, it stays out."

"Relax. It's not for me anyway."

"I don't care who it's for, just keep it out while we're working on my film."

Marcus nods and stares at me with his wicked eyes. Then, under his breath, he says, "You should be thanking me."

I'm not sure if he's talking about his dad's donations or his business with Will or what. I don't want to know. The dude is creepy and I just want to keep my distance.

Inside the film classroom, I take a seat. Riley plops in the chair next to mine and we wait for the others to join us. We used to make movies and work on projects during Film Studies. But now that the school is broke, the class has become a glorified movie-watching session. We have to save the real filmmaking for our club after school—the club without any funding. In addition to Marcus' donations, we resort to using my Sony video camera. Lucas, another senior and film diehard, uses the school leftovers and some of his own equipment for a pieced-together editing system, and Homer joins us when he can, but it's all on a volunteer basis.

Our skinny team of ragtag filmmakers consists of:

Director/Writer/Producer: Yours Truly
Editor: Lucas
Actors: Riley and Jonah
Key Grip: Caleb
Grips: Stella and Marcus

Thankfully, we also have a handful of production assistants and extras to jump in when we need them. In last year's film, we needed a ton of actors, so I stepped in. Riley and I played a couple who were totally into each other. It was the best three months of my life.

This year, our story is badass—a seven-minute short about an outcast girl's journey to popularity. She wins *the* boy by getting revenge on everyone who stands in her way. It's gritty, raw, and a bit twisted, with alternate dimensions of reality.

"Hanging in there?" I lean into Rye and squeeze her knee. I feel a little spark at the contact and wonder if she feels it too.

She nods and smiles. This time it doesn't look forced.

See, everything is going to be okay.

I can tell that Rye even spruced herself up for the shoot. Her hair falls over her shoulders like she's just brushed it and her shirt is crisp and different from the one she had on earlier. Usually, by this time of day, her clothes are crumpled and her hair is wrapped up in some kind of knot on her head that's held together by whatever she can find: pens and pencils, chopsticks, tiny paintbrushes. One time she actually had a fork shoved in there.

"Should we go over your scene since Jonah isn't here yet?" I ask her.

Though I'd prefer to be the actor in this piece, I don't want to give up directorial control. So I picked the least threatening person to be Riley's love interest: Jonah.

It's still hard to watch.

"Yes, please," Riley says, jumping up at my offer. "I can use all the help I can get."

We take our places.

"Ready, Rye?"

"Excuse me?" she says, hands on hips.

I always forget that she likes to be in character even while rehearsing. She's a little method that way.

"Sorry, *Ashley*," I say using her character's name. "All set?"

She gives me a thumbs-up and we're ready to pretend.

We go through the scene where reality meets fantasy: A distracted Ashley falls while getting out of her desk, spilling her books on the floor. Tim stops to help her up. I follow her through the bit, playing Tim as he starts to notice this beautiful, shy girl. My job is to watch her, help her with her books, and fall for her.

I do.

And it's not an act.

When we get to the part on the floor, where I put my arm around her and help her up, my hand rests on the small of her back—the exact place where her shirt was riding up the other day—and I'm instantly turned on. The one area where

I have no control? My own body. I shift my legs so that Rye can't see just how happy I am to be doing this scene with her.

Then Homer joins us.

That takes care of the problem at once.

Homer's carrying a box. His face is ashen, like he just saw a ghost. He sets the box down and waves me and Rye over.

"I just cleaned out some of Rach—I mean, Ms. Dunn's things from her classroom upstairs. We need the space. I know you both were close to her. Would you like any of this?"

I shake my head. I don't need a memento.

"I'd like to look," Riley says.

"Take it all, Riley." Homer sighs.

"No, just let me look. I don't want all of it."

"She would've wanted you to have it." Homer holds up his palms. "Please."

Rye nods and cradles the box like she's holding a newborn.

"So, how's the film coming along, Dez?" Homer switches gears.

"It's coming," I tell him.

"Thanks for your help," Riley says, taking her leave so I can give Homer an update on our progress.

After I bring him up to speed, Homer leaves us to it. I get everyone in place and we start rolling for the real deal. Riley and Jonah go through the scene while I film. I try to stay focused, but I can still feel Rye's skin on my fingertips. I have a hard time managing the camera.

Lucas watches over my shoulder. He's a little OCD and always wants me to overshoot. The guy wants to have his pick of angles and close-ups when he edits; he acts like he's the director. Lucas is one of the only guys *out* in school, and I've watched what he's had to go through because of it. The jokes and comments. The Tori Rollers' brainwashing—all in an effort to "save" him. The way the teachers just turn away from it all.

Now Riley is following in his footsteps.

I hate it. I was supposed to prevent all of this, and instead I've made it worse.

"I need a tight of their faces together," Lucas whispers in my ear.

As I set up the shot, he keeps saying, "Closer, closer."

"That's close enough," I bark, not liking the shot in my viewfinder and feeling like I'm losing control of everything. Jonah's face is almost touching Riley's and I can't help feeling like I want to break something. Or... someone.

"Stop being so uptight," Lucas says. "This movie is for the festival, not the church. I need these shots."

"I got this, Luke." I keep my voice steady. "Let's just try it this way. If we need more shots later, we'll get more shots."

Lucas pouts for a few seconds and then gives me my space.

Riley and Jonah finish the scene.

My way.

After we finally get everything we need, I call it. "That's it for tonight, guys. Nice job."

I pack up the equipment and drain my bottled water in two gulps. I hand my extra water to Riley and we walk out to the lot, to my ancient Beemer. Once upon a time it was red, but now it's so old and worn and faded that it almost looks pink. It still runs like a dream, and that's all I really care about. And since Rye doesn't have a car, it gives me the perfect excuse to spend more time with her.

When I open Riley's door, she drops into the seat in a puddle.

"Wanna stop off for coffee?" I ask, stalling for more time with her.

"No. I'm so tired I can't even see straight." She leans against the window with her eyes closed. "I just want my bed."

Ah! Don't go there.

I imagine her crawling into bed wearing her favorite sweatpants. The blue jobs with rips in the legs and the butt that's almost worn out. My breathing quickens just thinking about it.

Jesus, Dez. Get a grip.

"Come over later?" she asks.

"Yeah, I think I can make it," I say, knowing there's no place I'd rather be.

RILEY

In rehearsal, I try to shut out all the background noise when I move with Dez to the floor scene. It's easy to do, because Dez is totally in character. His hands are possessive when they wrap around me, and I feel something I can't place. Comfort? Happiness? Need? I fall into the scene with him, no longer noticing anything else in the room.

Except him.

His face is close to mine. I can smell his minty breath; it's cool on my face as he says Jonah's lines. It's nice, and I find myself imagining what it would be like to be with him. Not like it could happen. He has a girlfriend, a girl from film camp he met over the summer. Allie. He says things with Allie are casual and doesn't talk about her much. I've never met her—I've never met any of his love interests—but I have a feeling that with Allie, it's more than he lets on.

I've always been jealous when Dez tells me about the girls he's interested in. "What's she like?" I ask every time I find a girl's sweater in his car, or smell perfume on him after a date, or overhear a steamy phone call. Then I cringe when he gives me his standard response: "She's cool. You know, smart, pretty, nice body." And the worst part? The way he clears his throat before saying "nice body." In my mind, the girls look like supermodels with long wavy hair, curvy legs, flawless skin—completely perfect in their girliness. Still, I haven't figured out who it is that I'm jealous of. Is it the girls, for getting to be with Dez? Or is it Dez, for getting to be with the girls?

Too soon, Homer walks into rehearsal and breaks up our scene. My connection with Dez? Gone. I shake it off, realizing it was probably only in my head anyway. Homer drops a box on the desk and waves us over. A Degas statue sticks out of the cardboard and I know it's *hers*. Ms. Dunn collected all the Degas dancer sculptures.

Homer says we can have her things, but I only want a statue. I want that piece of her—proud and beautiful.

Then again, there might be clues in here.

I take the box of Ms. Dunn's things, careful not to disturb the contents.

That's when a memory flashes of her. That last day.

"Riley, I'd like to talk to you about one of your friends," she said. "I'm worried."

Now I wonder. Did she want to talk about Libby?

She looked concerned when she said it, but that's not what bothers me. There was something about the way she looked that day. The way she moved. I didn't realize it at the time, but looking back, I think she was anxious. Scared, even.

Ms. Dunn never did tell me what friend she wanted to talk about because that afternoon a huge group of girls came in with pictures of their homecoming dresses. She shrugged her shoulders and said we'd talk later. We never got the chance.

Once I have the box in my arms, I leave Dez with Homer. Then I hear the buzz. The same buzz that floated through the hallways for weeks after Ms. Dunn's murder, when everyone was weighing in on suspects:

I think it was that homeless guy who used to hang around the dumpsters.

Totally, he did it.

Nope, it was the janitor.

I think an old boyfriend did it.

Or maybe a girlfriend.

I snap my head around and the rumor mill comes to an abrupt stop. Then I try to sneak out to get a look inside the box. I only have a few minutes before we start filming.

Marcus catches me first.

"I always liked this one," he says as he reaches over to touch the Degas. His thumb skims across the statue.

I don't like him touching it. I want to keep her things pure. Or as pure as they can be, given that the police have already rifled through them. I set the box down next to my bag, pushing it out of his reach.

"So, Riley." Marcus smiles. "You and Emma? Finito?"

"What's it to you?" I look around the room for an excuse to get away from him. Homer and Dez are now in deep conversation and Jonah's not here yet, so I'm stuck.

"Well, I'm interested in Emma... and I want to make sure you're done tempting her with your... lady parts," he says.

He's honestly the most disgusting creature I've ever met.

"I'm done, Marcus," I say. "But from what I've heard, she won't be impressed by your little boy parts either."

He stands there, trying to form a comeback while I move onto the set to see if I can help the grips. They work on lighting and sound and get very little credit for any of it, so I always try to help out when I can. I notice Stella out of the corner of my eye. She's helping Caleb with the lighting. She doesn't say much, but I've noticed that Caleb is always asking her something. It's almost like she's the Key Grip—the one in charge—instead of him. She doesn't seem to mind that he takes the credit for her ideas. I like that about her—no ego issues.

I walk over to her as she positions one of the lights. "Anything I can do?" I ask.

She looks around. "Hmm, I don't think so. We seem to be in good shape."

I know it's stupid, but I want to help her with something. Like she did for me in gym class.

"Hey." I clear my throat. "I wanted to say thanks for speaking up for me."

"What?" Stella looks confused.

"In gym."

"Oh, that." She rolls her eyes. "Those girls are annoying."

"Yeah, they're the spawn of the devil," I say. "Don't let their *Jesus is my BFF* bumper stickers fool you."

"Amen." Stella giggles and her entire face lights up.

I shiver. She gives me goose bumps and I'm not sure why.

"Don't worry," Stella adds. "I can handle Tori. We work in the office together, so I know exactly how she operates."

Stella goes back to her lights and I take a seat next to Ms.

Dunn's things. I'm so anxious to open the box, I have to sit on my hands. I can't go through her stuff in front of the cast and crew. It wouldn't be right. So I wait, and pray that there's a clue inside.

DEZ

When we get home, Riley drags herself out of the car. She's sleepy and totally adorable. I lean against the trunk and watch her shuffle all the way across the yard to her door. The whole time I'm grinning like an idiot, excited we have plans tonight.

The cool air makes my nose run. That last little tease of warmth has gone and we're on the downward slide into winter. Across the street, Mrs. Andre has put the insulation film on her windows and now is blowing them with her hair dryer to tighten the plastic and get the wrinkles out. Mrs. Andre says her shrink-wrapped house saves her over one hundred dollars a month on her heating bill.

Winter preparation 101. This is how we roll in the Heights.

I walk over to give Mrs. Andre a hand with the windows on the second floor. I started helping her a few years ago to impress Riley, but now it's just become a habit. On the ladder—third rung from the top—I see Mrs. Andre holding the base. I can't say I'm comforted knowing that the only thing preventing me from a fall is a ninety-pound senior citizen, so I try to make fast work of it. I pull the wrap tight across the first window and seal it with a few waves of the blow dryer. It smells like burnt plastic. After a few more waves of hot air, the wrinkles disappear.

I seal up eight windows just before we run out of daylight.

"Oh, thank you, Desmond," Mrs. Andre says when I'm done. "You're such a nice young man."

If she only knew.

When I finally make it home, there's a package waiting for me on the stoop. I grab it and head inside—where it appears our house has thrown up Halloween. Orange and black cover every surface. Ever since Mom and Bernie got together, she's become one of those holiday junkies. It's funny because it wasn't always this way; Mom didn't always have an affinity for seasonal soap dispensers and themed tchotchkes. Especially when I was in fifth grade and she was with Phil, the manchild.

That year, I talked about my costume for weeks. I wanted to be Wolverine from the X-Men, but in a cool, Hugh Jackman kind of way. Furry face, wicked claws, wife-beater and jeans. I remember Mom had to wait for a check to clear or something and couldn't pick up the fur and claws until the 31st.

Turns out, that was the year she actually forgot Halloween … cue tearful childhood scene:

FLASHBACK SEQUENCE
INT. BRANDT HOUSE—HALLOWEEN

A 12-year-old DESMOND paces in the living room, waiting for his Mom.

The clock reads 6:00 when DEZ'S mom, TRUDY, finally enters.

DEZ
(smiling as he meets his mom at the door)
Finally! I thought we were going to miss trick-or-treating.

TRUDY
(sets her bag down and shakes her head)
Oh, honey.

DEZ
(looks behind his mom's back for the costume)
What? Where are the claws and fur?

TRUDY
I'm so sorry, Desmond. I don't have them. I can't explain it now but I'll make it up to you, I promise. Now, I'm sure we can find something here that you could wear.

DEZ looks at his mom in disbelief. He breaks down, yelling and crying. He runs up to his room and slams the door.

Minutes later, RILEY walks in and DEZ swipes at his face to hide his tears.

RILEY
What's up? You're not looking very wolveriney. Everything okay?

DEZ
She couldn't get the stuff. I can't go.

TRUDY enters the room, holding a pile of white sheets.

TRUDY
How about a ghost, honey? A classic ghost. They never go out of style.

DEZ falls back on his bed, hides his face, and groans in frustration.

RILEY
(starts taking off her Padmé Amidala Star Wars costume)
I love it. Dude, it's old school. A retro ghost, like from the old-time days.

DEZ
(looks up)
What are you doing?

RILEY
Think I'm going to let you steal all the retro glory? Nuh uh. I'm going as a ghost too.

END FLASHBACK

Amazingly enough, Riley and I had the best time that night. She was there for me in a way nobody else could be. And as I go up to my room, I finalize my plans to do the same for her this Halloween. I take the package that was delivered today and open it.

This will definitely work, I think, looking over the costume.

Yes. I'll put things in motion tomorrow. A Halloween party for the film crew. I can see the event play out already. I'd be the director: setting the scene, getting all the actors into place, telling the story. See, whether it's film or life, it doesn't matter. I want to be that one person in charge.

I wish I wasn't this way.

I wish I didn't crave control.

But I do . . . badly.

And though I might not be able to control Riley, I can help get her to where she needs to be. *Convince. Persuade. Protect.* This will be the night I make my move, and now that I'm in charge of my own costume, I'll no longer be that pathetic boy waiting to become a superhero.

I'll be playing the villain instead.

RILEY

After Dez drops me off, I hunker down at home. I go upstairs and take Ms. Dunn's box over to the window seat in my room. Outside, I can see Dez helping Mrs. Andre with her windows, just like he does every year. The trees, blowing in the breeze, are still holding on to half their leaves, but the green has given way to orange and it seems to make the sky glow around them.

The wind picks up, stirring the fallen leaves and blowing on all the campaign signs staked in the yards. Devlin's face expands and contracts all over our block. He's everywhere—watching.

You don't even see the signs for Roger Michelson—the only person brave enough to run against Devlin. Mr. Michelson owns the auto parts store in town. His heart is in the right place, but he's not cut out for politics. As far as our citizens are concerned, Devlin's got the election in the bag.

I open the box and take out Ms. Dunn's Degas statues one by one. The dancers are in various poses: an arabesque, fourth position, and one stands examining the sole of her foot. Ms. Dunn's initials are engraved on the bottom of each one. She loved these statues. They're just replicas, but she always said they reminded her of her childhood, sitting backstage while her mother danced. There's a statue missing, though. Ms. Dunn's favorite—The Little Dancer. I dig through the box but it's not in here. I remember playing with it while Dez was setting up the camera, that last day we filmed in her classroom.

Who would have taken it?

I continue to search through the box, and all that remains are books and CDs. I examine each item, hoping it will tell me something about who hurt her. It's intimate and personal and I feel like I shouldn't have this stuff. I'm just about to shut the box when I find the framed photograph of Ms. Dunn's parents, the one she proudly displayed on her shelf. She told me they died when she was sixteen. I don't think she ever got over it. She had no other family, and she never hung out in town with friends or even with other teachers. She was a loner. Our school was her life.

I have to bite the inside of my cheek to keep the tears at bay. I miss her so much.

The photo is black and white. Ms. Dunn's mom is dressed for the ballet, clad in toe shoes and a tutu, and her dad has his arms wrapped around her waist.

It's beautiful.

I bring it over to my own shelf and set it next to my collection of Audrey Hepburn movies. When I pull out the stand attached to the back of the frame, it wiggles.

I turn it over to secure it, and find a piece of yellow paper sticking out of the back. Carefully, I open the back of the frame.

And nearly a dozen papers flitter to the ground.

They're covered in names and dates. Notes to attorneys, school board minutes, correspondence with Ron Devlin.

I pour over every scrap of info. I don't understand all of it, but one thing is obvious: Ms. Dunn had to be scared to hide it.

"Chica!" Libby yells as she storms into my room.

She wakes me up and I jump, knocking the frame and papers to the floor. I've fallen asleep in my pile of clues. The nightmares are catching up with me.

"Sorry I'm a little early," she says. "I had to get out of the house. Our dinner tonight was something they'd have on the space shuttle. Most of it came from a powdered substance, Riley. *Powder.* Instant potatoes and fake gravy. Even the milk came from powder, if you can believe it. And then there was the vacuum-sealed mystery meat. I can't begin to tell you what it smelled like. I think my family has hit an all-time low."

I blink myself into the present as Libby talks. Once she comes into focus, I pick up Ms. Dunn's papers, throw everything in the box, and slide it under my bed.

There's no way Libby could be involved, and I feel so bad for even thinking it. She's had such a hard time at home.

"What's that?" Libby points to the box.

"Uh, nothing." I stand in front of my bed, guarding the clues.

"Right." She takes a step forward. "Come on, tell."

"Just some of Ms. Dunn's things." I keep my eyes glued to hers.

"Oh, why?" Libby plays it cool, not frazzled at all.

See, she didn't have anything to do with it.

"Homer wanted me to have her stuff. They finally cleaned out her classroom."

There has to be a perfectly good explanation for why Libby was there that day.

"Really." She flushes and swallows.

Or, maybe not.

Libby quickly changes the subject. "Well, forget about all that for tonight—we need to get moving." She claps her hands together. "We have plans, remember?"

I take inventory of her and immediately know what she has in mind. She's dressed in black from head to toe and has a bag of supplies.

"For real, Libby?" I crash into my pillow. "Dirty Deeds, tonight?"

I reach for my phone and it tells me I slept for over two hours. It also says I've missed three calls from Dez.

"Yes," Libby says. "I'm so itching for a little Tori revenge. Aren't you?"

When we were in junior high and had too much time on our hands, we came up with a new pastime called "Dirty Deeds"—it consisted of activities from TPing houses and stealing beer from garage refrigerators to other, more creative pranks. We like to bring back those good ol' days every now and then. For fun... or revenge. Tonight, however, I want to pass.

I break it to her. "I'm so not up for it. You go, have fun, send me a postcard."

"Nuh-uh," Libby says, pulling me upright. "Come on, I'm not letting you go all suicide hotline on me. You need to get out."

Ah, she thinks I'm upset because of Emma—but I haven't even thought of her tonight. Okay, I've *thought* of her but I haven't *obsessed* over her. It's Libby who has me stressed.

Knowing I won't win this battle, I grab my phone and put out the SOS, hoping Dez will pick up.

He does, so I put him on speaker.

"Dude, you need to help me," I tell him.

"Ah, *dude*," Dez says in his *I'm irritated but not going to admit it* tone. He hates when I call him "dude." "What happened? I thought we were going to hang out tonight."

"Sorry, I fell asleep, and now Libby is kidnapping me."

I don't want to ditch Dez. Still, I need to spend some time with Libby and find a way to ask her about the video. It's not just something I can bring up between classes at school.

Libby leans into my phone. "Dez, we need to do something, stat. Our girl here is depressed. She's even talking about going back to boys again, if you can believe it. This is serious shit."

I can't believe my ears. So much for discretion. I push

Libby away from the phone, killing her slowly with my death glare.

"What?" she whispers. "It's only Dez."

"Wait," Dez yells. "Riley, what is she talking about?"

I can hear Dez's stepdad, Bernie, in the background, "Stop yelling, Desmond. You know, you two are just like an old married couple."

"Uh, *privacy*?" Dez yells back. "Hey," he says into the phone. "What's going on?"

"Nothing," I tell him, trying to do damage control. "Libby's just being dramatic."

"Oh," Dez finally says. He sounds almost disappointed.

"Hey, why don't you come with us tonight?"

"I'm actually meeting Allie later," he says.

Right—Allie, the film camp girl. It's nice at least one of us has a love life. "This late?"

"Yeah, well, while you were sleeping, she called. Her parents are out of town for the night."

I close my eyes, not even wanting to think about what he has planned. I hate that I feel that twinge of jealousy again.

"You sure?" My voice is weak. Pitiful.

"Yeah. Look, I'll see you tomorrow, okay?"

He doesn't even wait for an answer before he hangs up.

Click.

Libby grunts. "That guy is so moody."

"Not moody," I say, defending him. "That's just Dez."

"Well, if you really decide to go back to boys, promise me one thing?"

"What?"

"That you won't date *him*."

"Why not?"

"He's too controlling, and I know I'd never get to see you."

Not controlling. He just doesn't trust you. "Don't worry. I don't think there's much chance of that happening."

"Good." Libby looks at me and grins. "Come on. Let's go."

I get up with a terrible feeling of dread. As much as I want to hang out with my friend and find out what she knows, get a little revenge on our resident mean girl, and forget about everything from the week, I can't help feeling that something bad's going to happen.

DEZ

Characters: Ken, Joan, and Riley Frost; and Riley's friend, Libby Jones.

Scene: The Frosts, out on the porch, seeing their daughter and her friend off for the night.

Mood: Tension. The parents are reluctant to let their daughter out at night after Ms. Dunn's murder. The girls work to ease their worries, but Riley has reservations of her own.

I hear them out on the porch. "Bye, Joan. Bye, Ken." Libby is bidding farewell to Riley's parents.

Kiss ass.

There's never been any love lost between me and Libby. We've never clicked, but we try, for Riley. Behind the scenes, we fight for her attention. I've even used Libby as my scapegoat a time or two. But she deserves it. She likes to see Rye down and out and she'll do just about anything for an ego boost. She tried putting the moves on me back in the day because she couldn't stand to see Riley getting all the attention. I kept that little episode to myself.

Slippery Libby.

Outside my bedroom window, I watch Rye lean in for her parents' goodbye kisses. She learned a long time ago that resistance is futile when it comes to their doting ways. The quicker she can get it over with, the better. After what happened with Ms. Dunn, they tightened the reign. They aren't the only ones. The Heights used to be a place where nobody locked their doors, where you could walk anywhere at night, where there was always someone around who had your back. Ms. Dunn's murder changed all that.

Joan and Ken linger outside, and the girls indulge them for a few minutes until Libby puts her arm around Riley and slowly pulls her off the porch. If she didn't, the Frosts would keep them there all night. Riley brushes a stray hair from her face, one that's escaped the knot she's tied on top of her head. I move a little closer to my window and watch.

They leave, and I'm left alone in my room, so I pick up my camera.

Instead of pining over Rye, this is how I should be spending my time. If I want to get into Columbia, I have to do more than hang in my room like a recluse. I need a film, a kick-ass one, to get the scholarship I need for the insane Ivy League price tag.

After the film festival, Riley and I are both going to New York for college interviews and auditions. Our official letters finally came in the mail. Riley's applying to Tisch at NYU. I'm putting all my eggs in the Columbia basket. Only a subway ride apart. For Rye, Tisch is her second choice. Her first is the U of M Guthrie program here at home. She wants to keep the cost down for her parents. Tisch would be better for her and everyone knows it, but once again, it's going to be up to me to do the convincing.

I flip open the viewfinder and turn on the camera—the only thing that will take my mind off my obsession with Riley. I can spend hours playing with shots and scenes and sequences. Just for practice. I haven't done it in a few weeks. Not since I accidently taped Rye and Emma in the car.

I was hanging out my window, camera in hand, working on perspective shots when a car pulled into the Frosts' driveway. I thought I could capture a scene in real time, so I zoomed in.

To Riley and Emma.

Kissing.

A disturbing scene that continues to replay, over and over in my head.

Riley.

With Emma.

It makes me ache.

At first, I thought Riley was faking the whole gay thing, trying to be a rebel or eccentric or something. Junior high was when it started getting weird. We'd both notice the same girl walking by and we'd both blush when we got caught, or we'd put on the same cocky show in front of someone we liked.

That's when Riley decided to like girls and there was nothing I could do about it—which made me want her even more. Completely fucked up, I know.

By the time high school started, she seemed to grow out of it, like I'd said she would. It didn't last.

When she told me she was interested in girls again, I pulled away. It was too hard. But after hearing about what went down in my cousin's school in Iowa, I was worried for her. My cousin Adam said it was really bad at his school. Sick shit—like homophobes stripping gay guys' clothes off and duct-taping them in the locker room, posting nasty pictures and videos all over the Internet, spray-painting their cars.

They weren't any easier on the girls.

Then came the suicides. One after another. All gay kids.

I vowed that I'd never let anything like that happen to Riley.

My phone goes off for like the fifth time in the last hour. I don't even look at it. I know it's Jonah. He wants me to double again this weekend, but I just can't go through another night with Nicole. No way.

There's only one person I want to talk to tonight, so I punch in the number.

It rings five times. There's no answer or voicemail—not like I'd leave a message anyway. Texting is out of the question too. I guess I'll just have to try again later.

I go back to my camera and study the shots from rehearsal. I like how they look. The story is taking shape. I look at the script and make a few edits. But it's Libby's words that I can't get out of my head. I can't stop thinking about them.

Did Riley really say she's going back to boys?

Was Libby exaggerating?

What's really going on?

I hit redial on my phone.

"Hello, Desmond," the voice vibrates on my ear.

"Hey, just checking in. Any news?" I ask with a cringe. I hate betraying Riley this way, but it has to be done.

"No news is good news."

"Meaning?" I ask.

"They won't dare talk to each other, and my people tell me there's been no contact."

"Your people?" I roll my eyes.

"How else do you think I get things done around here? This is not a one-person operation."

"Oh, I think I have a pretty good idea of how you work. But remember, your job is to keep Riley and Emma apart, not to make Rye's life difficult."

"Beggars can't be choosers, Dez. You wanted my help, remember?"

This was a mistake.

"Yeah, I remember," I say, trying to even my voice. "But don't forget that I helped you too. I'm not the only one here with something to lose."

"Dez, you *don't* want to play with me."

"Just lighten up on Riley," I say quickly before I hang up.

Shit, what have I done?

In the corner of my room, the Godfather looks down from his perch on the wall and says, *Now there's somebody who knows how to do business.*

RILEY

We keep our eyes glued on the Devlins' windows. Tori and her younger sisters are doing homework at the kitchen table while their mother does the dishes. Papa Devlin is reading the newspaper.

"Okay, it's my turn," I say to Libby, opening my hand for our weapon of choice.

She hands me the remote control.

I take it like a wand, and presto. The TV in the Devlins' basement turns on and the volume slowly climbs to full blast.

I give Libby a quick wink—it's a fun game.

Mr. Devlin lifts his head up from the paper and stands up. He looks like he's yelling something, but we can't make out what it is. I choke back a giggle. Through the windows, we watch as Devlin stomps down into the rec room and turns off the TV. He checks it over, flips it on and off a few times, and heads back up stairs. When he sits down and pulls up his paper, I flick my wand again, turning on the downstairs TV with the volume blaring.

Libby is doubled over with laughter, slapping my thigh.

The whole family looks at each other, scratching heads and waving arms. And *that* seems to make the whole scene even funnier. This time they all go downstairs and huddle around the TV. I wish Dez was here to see it.

Although I've become the master of the game, I've got to give it up for Libby, who invented Remote Control Revenge one boring summer night. It's become one of our favorite Dirty Deeds. In RCR, we stake out an area with some of our least favorite residents. We come armed with TV remotes—with only one cable company in town, the remotes are pretty universal—and we find the living room window where we can see our neighbors watching their favorite evening television show, and then bam . . . we change the channel. They never know what hit them.

It's good, clean fun.

I've added a few of my own signature moves to the game, like turning on random TVs throughout the house and watching the people scatter. The volume control is another one of my moves. Yeah, it's immature and silly, but also extremely entertaining.

The Devlins continue to mess with the TV, and that's when I see it. I take Libby's binoculars and zoom in. There on the shelf is a ballerina. Little Dancer.

Ms. Dunn's missing Degas.

My breath catches and I lose the Degas in the lenses, but something else comes into view. It's Devlin in the window, staring back at me.

He's figured it out.

"Run," Libby whispers.

We leap off the picnic table and Libby motions for me to follow. We head through the neighbors' yards until we're almost a block away.

Libby deftly navigates our route. "Watch out for the rose bushes," she whispers.

Too late. The branches graze my arms, taking quick bites from my shoulder down to my wrist.

In the distance, I hear a light trickling sound. It's running water. The creek.

The creek leads to the Clay Hole, a small pond that developed after clay diggers hit a spring about a million years ago. It's our only real swimming area in town, but only the lower end of the food chain uses it. Dez and I lived there when we were kids.

As we run through the woods, we close in on the creek. "Time to jump," Libby whispers back to me.

We take a running start and leap across the water, clearing it with ease. We're officially on the other side of the tracks now. The creek separates Devlins' neighborhood from the rest of our city's riffraff.

"There's a shed back here," Libby says. "Come on."

How does she know what's back here?

Libby seems oddly familiar with the area. That's when I realize we're almost at Ms. Dunn's house. We start running again. Branches and leaves skim our bodies as we fly through the trees. As we slow down, the tiny hairs on the back of my neck stand at attention. I hear footsteps getting closer.

We slip into the decaying shed. I crouch down behind

an old bench and Libby hides under a table in the back. There are gardening tools and old pots leaning against the walls. I try to catch my breath but hold it again when the shed door squeaks and begins to open.

The moonlight shines through the broken window and a shadow grows on the wall. A huge shadow. It's like a scene from a corny old horror film. I can't look. Instead, I squeeze my eyes shut and bite my lip.

That's when a hand clamps down on my shoulder.

The hand grabs me and I jump, holding in a scream.

It's Devlin. The killer.

The hand flips me around.

I can't make out the face, but Libby can.

I've completely forgotten that she's been here the entire time.

"Jake," she says, her voice low and quiet. "What are you doing out here?"

We know Jake Noring from school, so my heart rate automatically slows, yet I have to remind myself that no one's to be trusted.

Libby's had a crush on Jake since seventh grade, but nothing's ever come of it. He lives on the nice side of town and spends his time playing traveling soccer on a city team. Libby doesn't exactly run in the same circle and, despite what she says, I think she'd like to.

Oh no. Was that Jake's voice on the video? Libby's partner in crime?

"Shhh," he whispers. "He's coming. Let's get out of here."

I try to remember the voice on the video, but I can't tell if it was him. I don't know if I should stay or run.

Jake leads us out the door and within seconds we're running through the woods again. We run until we're out of breath, then duck down among the downed trees. I suddenly feel like I have to pee. We wait there, crouched in the woods, hiding.

My legs are shaking so badly I have to lean forward on my knees. I can't believe I'm stuck in the woods surrounded by murder suspects.

"What are you doing out here?" I ask Jake, since he didn't answer Libby the first time.

"I saw you behind the Devlins' house," he says. "I live next door to them, ya know."

I didn't remember that, but obviously Libby did. That's why she kept staring off.

"I was coming out to scare you guys when Devlin started hauling ass in your direction." He laughs.

I can't believe I saw the missing Degas in the Devlin house. Maybe the mayor is like one of those serial killers and the statue is his trophy after killing Ms. Dunn.

Once again, my brain is on overdrive. I need to get back into that house. There has to be a way to find out if Devlin's involved.

"I've heard about your little remote control trick," Jake says, interrupting my scheming. "Pretty clever."

"Thank you very much." Libby beams.

"So now what's on the agenda? Tormenting any of my other neighbors tonight?"

"Nope, I think that's it," Libby says. "We're in my neck of the woods now. Are you mad?"

"Not even close. Anytime someone can stick it to the Devlins, especially Tori, I'm all for it."

Tori. That's it. She's my ticket into the house.

"Really?" Libby's hope is seeping through her pores.

"Really," he says. "So, where to now?"

God. I can't take it anymore. "Do you guys want to save your flirting until maybe we don't have a pissed-off mayor after us?"

Libby glares at me.

"Relax, Riley," Jake says. "If Devlin hasn't made it here by now, he's not going to."

Yeah, but maybe he's not the only one I'm worried about.

Libby and Jake continue to flirt and I continue to study Jake's voice.

"We were just heading to the coffee shop," Libby says.

We were?

"Wanna come?" she asks.

"Sure." Jake shrugs.

And just like that, I'm the third wheel.

We sneak into Libby's car, which is strategically parked on the dirt road behind the woods. I watch Libby and Jake for any signs or trip-ups, but soon I just want to get away from them.

I fake cramps and make Libby bring me home. I need to be alone to think.

I'm beginning to feel like I'm trapped in a cheesy whodunit movie and I can't get out. I'm the idiot girl trying to solve the mystery—the girl who puts herself in danger at every turn. The girl who opens the door—or pulls back the shower curtain or runs up the stairs—instead of running away from the killer. Except this is the Heights and until Ms. Dunn was killed, nothing remotely dangerous has ever gone down here. The police chief would say our little community is still just as safe. But if that's true, why are people putting new locks on their doors and sticking to a self-enforced curfew?

The clues continue to pile up, and if Devlin is involved, maybe that means Libby did nothing wrong. All I know is I have to find out the truth. The only way to do that is to investigate Devlin . . . which means I need to get closer to Tori.

And I think I know just how to do it.

DEZ

A beam of light rides across my room, moving my attention away from the disturbing phone conversation and over to the Frosts' house.

It's Riley.

Fuck.

My lights are on.

Why is she back so early?

She's seen me, I'm sure of it. I messed up. Now she'll know I was lying about hanging out with Allie.

My first mistake.

I flick off the light and move away from the window, onto the floor, crawling around like the dirty rat I am. There's nothing I can do about it now but make up a lie. Another one to add to my web. Yes, I've officially become a lying A-hole who has to make up shit because his life is so pathetic.

Truth is, there's no Allie. There never was. There's never been anyone I really wanted to be with.

Except Riley.

I've actually planted girls' clothes in my car and room. I've had fake phone conversations. I've even bought perfume to put on after my alleged dates. Of course, I know how psycho this all sounds. But it seemed that if Riley thought there was someone else in my life, she'd be more interested in me. It always works in the movies.

Who am I kidding? This is not the movies. Actually, all of this is reading more like a lame made-for-TV special and I'm dangerously close to jumping the shark. I need to wake the hell up and come back to the real world.

I can't make my surprise move at a fake Halloween party orchestrated in the hopes she'll fall into my arms. It doesn't work that way. Plus, this whole secret-crush thing has been going on for so long that I can't tell her the truth now, and I surely can't just come out and tell her how I feel about her. It's too late to do this like a normal guy would. I've completely fucked up.

I crawl over to my bed, pull the costume down, crunch it in a ball, and throw it in the trash. If it's going to happen between Riley and me, she's going to have to figure it out on her own.

It's the only way.

RILEY

On Saturday, we shoot on location at the city square in the Heights. We all pile into Caleb's old VW camper, with a group of extras following in the car behind, and set up in the park. Dez and I used to come down here with our families when we were kids. In the center of the park, under the clock tower, there used to be concerts. Flowers hung in baskets on the fence posts, and the grass was covered in a rainbow of blankets with people picnicking and listening to music.

Now the park is covered in weeds. Leaves have fallen and nobody's bothered to clean them up. The clock stays permanently frozen at 10:20 because there's no money to fix it.

"Wait in here, Rye," Dez says when I try to get out of the camper to help. "You're the star, remember?" He winks.

I try to smile back, but the papers I found in Ms. Dunn's photo frame weigh on my mind. They're in my bag right now and I so want to show them to Dez, but something won't let me.

I need more information *before* I bring Dez into this.

The square is quiet. It used to be buzzing with people doing their shopping and dropping kids at the fields for soccer practice. Today there are only a few residents eating at the local greasy spoon. Inside the diner, I can see the Devlins. The happy family is having breakfast together. With Coach K.

Figures.

Dez moves over to see what I'm looking at.

"I should've known," I tell him.

"What?" he asks.

"The reason Coach K never says anything to Tori when she calls me a dyke."

"What do you mean? He's actually heard her say that?"

Sometimes Dez can be so naive. "Oh yeah," I say. "He's even made a few cracks himself."

"He *what*?!" Dez's face turns red.

I can't believe I never told him this. "He makes jokes all the time, but I just chalked it up to his redneck nature. I didn't realize how tight he was with the Devlins."

I start to wonder just how many teachers Tori's dad has in his back pocket.

Dez takes out his camera and starts shooting the scene in the diner.

"Dez." I motion for him to put the camera down. "What are you doing?"

"Just getting some b-roll. You never know when you'll need it."

Exactly, I think, making sure the DVD of Libby in Ms. Dunn's room is still safe in my bag.

On Monday, I see Tori in the school garden, getting everything in place for the dedication. There's a new tree there, and the plaque to honor Ms. Dunn. Tori is actually weeding the neglected beds.

It's the perfect opportunity to make the first move. Especially since last week I overheard her talking to the Rollers about her church project…

> *"I have to help someone with their testimony and I'm running out of time," Tori said in her usual bitchy way. "Dad wants me to make a big deal of it at church—have me show how I helped some poor lost soul find God and change their life."*
>
> *"It's not like you haven't been looking, Tori," Natalie said. "I'm sure your dad will understand."*
>
> *"You are such a moron sometimes," Tori hissed. "Have you met my dad?"*
>
> *"Well, there's always Will," Paige offered. "I'm sure your dad would be impressed if you helped the biggest drug dealer of the school find the Lord."*
>
> *"Okay, there's one. I need a few more options."*
>
> *"What about Emma?" Natalie asked, trying to redeem herself.*
>
> *Tori nodded.*

The Rollers volunteered a few more names and Tori created her list.

I hadn't really thought about that conversation until after Devlin chased us on Friday night. It was then that I realized what I have to do. I need to get close to Tori—and the Degas statue—and what better way than to become her new pet project? Surely she'd jump at the chance to save a sinner like me.

I take a few steps into the garden, toward Tori. "Here." I grab the pile of weeds and throw them in the trash bag. "Let me help."

"My, that's awfully Christian of you, Riley."

"Yeah, well, this might surprise you, but I'm a Christian. I was raised Lutheran, Tori. Even confirmed."

"Really?" she asks, genuinely surprised. "I never would've guessed, especially considering your ... *choices*."

Choices. I ignore the fire igniting in my belly and keep a smile on my face. Yes, of course I *chose* to become the pariah of the school. Who wouldn't?

"Yeah, it's complicated," I say, trying to unclench my jaw.

"No, Riley, it's quite simple," she says in her most pious voice. "Leviticus 20:13: *If a man also lie with mankind, as he lieth with a woman, both of them have committed an abomination: they shall surely be put to death; their blood shall be upon them.* The Bible is perfectly clear on the matter."

"Maybe. But haven't you also heard, *the heart wants what it wants*?"

"Let me guess—a quote from a movie? You film club people are so weird." She rolls her eyes.

"Emily Dickinson, actually." I grab a rake. "Seriously, though, I meant it the other day when I said I was going to make a change. I'm done with girls. Now, do you want my help with this garden or not?"

If I pull this off, I should win an Oscar.

"I could use it," she says, wiping sweat off her otherwise perfectly made-up face. "If this isn't perfect for the ceremony, my dad will have a fit."

"Okay, I'm in."

DEZ

WEEKEND MONTAGE
ESTABLISHING SHOT—EXTERIORS OF THE FROST AND BRANDT HOMES

CUT TO: SPLIT SCREEN

Montage of RILEY on the right side of screen; montage of DEZ on the left. We see them both come into their rooms after Saturday's video shoot and plop down on their beds. Camera moves in on both of their faces as they are lost in thought. The scenes move in compressed time, showing them watch TV, read, and eat. DEZ plays with his video camera; RILEY reads her script. DEZ texts RILEY. RILEY quickly texts back. More texts and calls come in for RILEY, but she ignores the calls and shoves the phone under her mattress.

After Saturday's video shoot, I didn't see Riley the rest of the weekend and she only responded to my texts with one-word answers. This is pretty much her MO after a breakup.

She hides.

I sulk.

In the lunchroom today, Jonah sits at our table in the corner, his plate piled high with spaghetti. I make my way over to the pizza line.

"Hey, Dez." Glory brushes up against me as I wait.

I know she's here to shoot the shit. Girls like Glory don't eat pizza.

"So, what did you think of my performance the other day?" she asks, sticking out her boobs.

Glory is one of our extras for the film. She must be bored again. Glory is all hot and heavy about a guy who doesn't even know she exists—a senior named Jacob. And much like me, she's always looking for a distraction.

"You were great." I appease her because I know what it's like to crave attention. "But you do need to learn how to take direction," I add, teasing her. She had a heck of a time with blocking during our shots.

"Yeah, I know." She laughs. "I just like to get a rise out of you." She touches my arm and holds it there so that I get the hint.

In reality, Glory has gotten more than a rise out of me.

A few times.

The first was when Riley got together with Reed before sophomore year. Reed took up all Riley's free time that summer, leaving me alone. One lonely night, I ran into Glory at

Java and she made her move. I (graciously, I like to think) accepted. Something I consider doing again until I see Riley walk into the cafeteria. I move up the line, hardly listening as Glory talks, and order two slices.

"Glory," I tell her. "I can't do this right now." There's no point in beating around the bush.

"Oh." She pulls her chest in and looks down. "Well, if you change your mind, you know where to find me."

"Sorry," I say, and I mean it. She's a good egg. She's sweet and pretty and funny, but there's Riley. "See you later," I say before giving her a quick peck on the cheek.

I get my pizza and take a seat next to Jonah while Rye goes through the burger line.

"So, did you rekindle with Glory over the weekend?" Jonah asks. "Is that why you ignored my calls?"

"No and no," I say, my eyes glued to Riley.

"Well, what were you doing then? I really needed my wingman."

I tear my eyes away from Riley for a minute.

"Sorry pal, but I think it's time for you to fly solo." I bump his shoulder. "You are ready, young Jonah."

Riley interrupts my pep talk, setting her burger and Dr. Pepper on the table.

"Hey babe, how was the rest of your weekend?" I ask in between bites of pizza. "I didn't hear from you after the shoot."

Riley just shrugs as she dresses her burger in pickles and ketchup.

It's nice to have her back at our table, even if she's a little removed. Riley and Emma always used to sneak away for lunch, leaving me with Jonah and random members of the film crew. Occasionally, one of Jonah's friends from youth group would join our little lunch soirée for some real fun.

It sucked.

Riley watches as Emma grabs a cookie and milk and rushes out the side door.

"You know you're too good for her." I can't help but say it. I touch my hand to Riley's for a second. "She didn't deserve you."

And that's a cold hard fact. Emma lives a lie. She's gay and in the closet—and Jonah and I have been sworn to secrecy about the whole thing. She was so not worthy. Anyone who would keep Riley a secret doesn't deserve her.

If Rye was mine, I'd shout it from the rooftops.

"Dez." Riley shakes her head and slams her pop, wincing as it goes down her throat. "Can we not talk about it?"

"Yeah, of course." I try to ignore the pain in her eyes. "Sorry."

"What about you?" she asks.

"What about me?" I say, trying not to look guilty. I roll my second piece of pizza like a burrito and take a massive bite.

"I never got the chance to ask you what happened with Allie over the weekend. I noticed you didn't go out on Friday night."

Busted.

"Allie?" Jonah interrupts, confusion washing over his face.

Oh, shit.

I hold up a finger and finishing chewing while I send Jonah a look: *Bro code, man. Bro code.*

Jonah gets it and clams up.

"Her parents had a change of plans," I finally answer.

Now it's time for a quick diversion. I push my plate away and turn toward Jonah. "What about you?" I ask. "Tell us about your weekend with Ginger."

It's the perfect distraction technique. Pressure's off me and onto Jonah. Though Riley looks skeptical, she never asks me any more about the Allie situation because we spend the rest of our lunch giving dating advice to Jonah.

Score one, Desmond.

A BAD, BAD THING

INT. THEATER PROP STORE, SUMMER BEFORE SOPHOMORE YEAR—DAY

Inside the store, 15-year-old RILEY has her dark hair pulled into two messy Princess Leia buns and wears a T-shirt and camouflage shorts. She plays around with fake guns and weapons, acting out various movie fight scenes.

DEZ, also 15 years old, is tall and lean, with unkempt hair and a handsome face. He's lying on the floor watching Riley play with the props. He smiles at her longingly and we know immediately he has feelings for her. The two are out buying props for their high school film project—a story about gangsters.

RILEY
(puts the machine gun
under DEZ'S chin)
We're going to be late.
You better call your mom.

DEZ pulls his phone out from his
pocket and looks at the screen.

DEZ
(turns the phone around so
RILEY can see it)
My phone's dead.

RILEY
(reaches in her bag for
her new phone)
DUDE, you really need to get
your S-H-I-T together. Your
phone is always dead.

DEZ
(takes RILEY's phone)
And? That's some big crime?

RILEY
(waves the gun around and jokes)
People have been killed for less.

DEZ makes the call to his mom and tells
her they're going to be late.

RILEY
(continues evaluating the props)
Will you text Homer too? I'm supposed to be at rehearsal tonight.

DEZ
(messes with the phone)
I can't find Homer's number.

CUT TO:

CLOSE UP: PHONE CONTACT LIST

CUT TO:

WIDE SHOT: RILEY AND DEZ

RILEY
Oh, yeah, my contacts didn't transfer over. Look under recent calls. He's in there. It's the 636 number. Tell him I can't make it because I'm shopping with you.

DEZ finds the number, types the message, and hits send. He sets the phone down in front of him while Riley moves behind a rack of costumes.

The phone buzzes, so DEZ picks it up.

CUT TO:

CLOSE UP: PHONE SCREEN

The message is from RILEY's boyfriend, REED. DEZ realizes he accidently sent the text to Reed instead of Homer.

DEZ
(whispers)
Shit, wrong 636 number.

CUT TO:

CLOSE UP: PHONE SCREEN
Reed's text message says: Are we still on for tomorrow?

RILEY
(yells from behind the rack)
What's that?

DEZ
Oh nothing, just talking to myself.

DEZ looks around and types back: Sorry, can't make it.

He hits send. Then he deletes the entire text message exchange.

RILEY

In gym my plan starts to take hold. Tori tells Coach K that I'm joining her foursome for doubles.

She's picked me for badminton.

And maybe also for her church project.

"Fine." Coach barely looks up and sends us to the first net.

I take a quick glance at Libby before I follow.

"What the hell?" Libby mouths.

I shrug and follow my new bestie.

"Riley, I've been thinking." Tori links her arm through mine. "I could help you, you know? Help you work through your unnatural urges."

"What do you mean?" I play dumb. This is what I was banking on; I'm exactly the project she's been looking for.

"Well, if you're willing and committed, I could help get you on the right path."

"You could?" I ask, putting on my best innocent face.

"How?" It's the face I use on my parents when I'm trying to get out of something. It works like a charm.

"Well, the first step would be to welcome you into our fold." Tori waves her arms at the Tori Rollers behind us. Natalie, Paige, and Alexa all smile and nod. "We'll pray together and help show you the way."

"You'd do that?" I stifle the evil laugh that wants to escape. This is going to be easier than I thought.

"Of course I would. That's what our movement is all about. The Day of the Righteous is not just about one day. It's about helping people in need at any time. What do you say?"

I stop and look at her straight in the eyes. "I say *yes*."

"Yay." Tori places my hand in hers and extends the other out to the Rollers. "Quick prayer, girls. Bring it in."

The girls join us to create a linked circle. They all bow their heads and close their eyes.

I look around, half expecting a wind to pick up and the lights to flicker.

"God of mercy," Tori begins. "You have called on us to help lead Riley on the path of righteousness. Please help us in your mission. Please allow Riley to acknowledge her sins and help us all live by Christ each and every day. In his name. Amen."

The girls echo, "Amen." Then Tori leans in and whispers, "Don't worry, Riley. We'll pray away the gay."

I'm dying to ask just how that works but instead, I say my own little prayer.

Please, God, let this be over soon.

The next morning, I take it up a notch. If I'm going to play the part, I need to look the part. I page through a fashion magazine I picked up, and the glossy pages invite me into a new world. One where boys like girls and girls like boys.

I sneak into Mom's bathroom, grab a few tubes and bottles, and lock myself in my room. It's too early for my parents to be up, but I take no chances.

The sun shines through my window. The fall leaves have peaked—all yellows and golds of the birches, reds of the maples, orange of the oaks. Unfortunately, it won't last long. Soon they'll turn that deep shade of cinnamon, burnt leaves in a final burst before they fall. That's how I feel—my old self falling away like the leaves so that I can begin anew.

I rest on the floor, surrounded by lotions and potions, with magazine photos ripped out and taped to my mirror. I use the photos as a guide and take out Mom's pink bottle of Maybelline mascara. I pump the wand and go to work. Slowly, I take the tiny brush and run it up the length of my lashes. First the top, then the bottom.

It feels heavy when I blink but the reflection blinking back looks all right, so I keep going.

So far, so good.

When I study my eyes in the mirror, I can see that my lids are covered in tiny black dots from my lashes brushing up against them. I wet a Q-tip in my mouth and swab them clean. Then I take a huge makeup brush and dab it in Mom's translucent powder. I paint in wide strokes across my forehead, down my nose to my chin. It tickles and some of the powder gets in my nose, making me sneeze.

Once my eyes clear, I can see the results. It's not so horrible.

Next, I assess the selection of lip color. We have lipstick, lip liner, lip gloss, and lip stain in various shades of berry, brown, and nude. That's the one funny thing about Mom, my liberal, green, feminist mother. She's simple and principled and all that, but the lady goes to great lengths to look good. And, given this sampling of makeup, I'd say someone has a bit of a cosmetics addiction going on.

I look over all the choices and settle on the nude gloss. I take the tube and squeeze out a shiny bead the size of a pea and smear it on. My lips feel goopy and I have the strangest feeling they're going to be sealed shut if I keep my mouth closed for too long.

I study my closet and decide to swap my tennies for a pair of boots. Mom picked them up at a consignment shop last year. *They were never worn,* she said before telling me how much they go for at the store. I tried wearing them once and they killed my feet. But if I'm going to become a *real* girl, sore feet is a small price to pay. I tuck my leggings into my boots, throw on a shirt without a hood, and call it good.

It's funny, though. As I walk through the halls at school, I get a few raised eyebrows and even more smiles than normal.

It feels like I did something right.

"All right, Frost, what's going on?" Libby corners me in the hallway. "I leave you alone for a minute and you suddenly become one of Tori's clones?"

Think fast.

"I'm playing a part." I motion with my head so she'll come closer.

"And what part is that? Bible-thumping Barbie?"

"Our film for the festival, remember? Dorky girl turns into Cinderella? I need to see how the other half lives to get this right."

"But you hate Tori and . . . " Libby wipes my cheek with her thumb. "And makeup."

"It's for my art," I tell her, but she's not amused. She lets out a huff and rushes off to class.

During gym, things don't improve. When Libby overhears Tori inviting me to her annual Halloween party, she shoots flaming daggers at me with her eyes.

I brush her off.

Tori tells me there will be games and food and a bonfire outside, but all I'm thinking is that there will also be plenty of time to look around for evidence against her scumbag dad. And that's when I realize I need backup. I have to come clean to Dez; he'll know what to do.

I say "yes" to Tori's invitation, already plotting my next move, and practically skip into the locker room.

DEZ

It's the shoot I've been dreading. The major love scene. I snap orders and everyone complies, but I can tell they're trying to steer clear of me. I call for the actors. It's a cool thing, being in charge of people this way. Telling them what to do and how to do it. Plus, I'm good at it. And not just on screen.

That first time I started messing with Riley's love life, the guilt consumed me. I couldn't look her in the eyes for weeks. Yet after I erased that text message on her phone, it somehow felt like I'd done the right thing. I felt it in my gut. In a fucked-up way, I was actually *helping* her.

When Riley tried talking to Reed again, after the texting fiasco, he blew her off. Then Libby made her move on Reed. Of course, she denies it, but I saw them together. Rye never knew what hit her and the romance with Reed was over before it ever really started. She was crushed, but I made it up to her. I was there with flowers and food, and I listened. I listened to what she wanted, what she hoped for, and that's what I've tried to become for her.

It sounds a little crazy, I'll admit, but Reed didn't deserve Riley. He had no idea what kind of person she is—beyond the superficial. He would never have appreciated her like I do. Nobody can.

Riley and Jonah take their places and I say, "Action."

Rye oozes with confidence. Jonah's a little more reluctant until they get into the scene. Then it flows easily. Riley has *become* Ashley—bold, cool, and totally into boys. My stomach twists when she goes in for the kiss. I'm completely captivated. Jonah is trapped in her gaze. She slowly closes in, and when her lips meet his, he doesn't hold back. He dives in, and his hands travel all over her back.

I want to look away. It's torture. I don't know what's gotten into Riley, but I don't like it. I didn't even know she knew *how* to kiss like that. And Jonah? He's worse.

"Jesus, Jonah!" I yell. "Slow down. You're supposed to kiss her, not make a meal of her."

Everyone laughs and Rye looks particularly pleased.

I fight my way through the scene, and I'm relieved when we're finally walking to my car.

"So, you were into the scene today." I try to keep my voice casual. "A little *too* into it."

"Really?" She smirks. "Can you be *too* into a scene?"

"Well, think of Jonah. You almost gave the guy a stroke."

She laughs, clearly proud of herself.

"Come on, Rye, what's going on with you? I also heard that you and Tori were all cozy today."

That's what really has me on edge. What's with Tori's sudden personal interest in Rye? It's the last thing I need.

"Yeah, I know," she says. "I think I'm going to have a lot of people pissed at me."

"For what?"

"For what I'm about to do."

"And what's that?" I don't like the sound of this.

She looks around, trying to decide if she should tell me. She scoots close. "Can you keep a secret?"

She hauls me back into the school, to the edit suite, and pulls a DVD and a folder from her bag, gently placing them on the table.

"Can I show you something?" she asks.

"'Course," I say. "Let's see what you've got."

"You've got to promise me—this stays between us. No matter what."

"Okay, Rye. I promise."

Riley puts the DVD into the drive and hits play. It's that scene she made us reshoot.

"Why do you have this on DVD?" I ask.

"Because I deleted the file off the computer."

"Why?"

"If you'd shut up for a minute, I'll show you."

She fast-forwards to the end of the scene, but the footage keeps rolling. I must've forgotten to turn it off when we finished. Then I hear it. This is why she brought me here.

I listen as Libby and some guy talk about a stash Ms. Dunn had.

"Must be Will," I tell Riley. "He's the only one I know who buys synthetic drugs online."

"How do you know that?"

"How do we know anything around here?" *We look into our stepfather's police database.* "People talk, Riley."

"I mean, how do you know he was talking about synthetic drugs?"

"Why else would he be so worried about something being traced back to him?"

"Makes sense, I guess." Riley's lost in thought, tapping on the table.

"So you found this the day we were reviewing the tape?"

Riley nods.

"And that's why you wanted to reshoot?"

Another nod.

Nice.

"Why didn't you tell me earlier?"

"Because I knew you'd assume the worst about Libby."

"Well, it doesn't look good, Rye."

"That's not all," she adds, holding up a folder. "These were hidden in one of Ms. Dunn's picture frames." She opens the folder and pulls out a bunch of papers. "There could be clues in here, Dez. I think these might tell us who killed her."

"Didn't the police already go through Ms. Dunn's things?"

"Well, they obviously didn't see the video, and all of this stuff was hidden." Riley flicks the contents of the folder with her fingers and the papers flitter to the ground.

I snatch them up almost as fast, and Rye grabs my arm. Her eyes fill and my heart aches.

"Ms. Dunn was scared, Dez. She knew something."

"Maybe we should give it to the police now."

"No, we can't. Libby would be toast if we did."

"Rye, I really think the person who killed Ms. Dunn is long gone."

"No. I think that person has been right here the entire time."

"You're playing with fire. I don't think we should get involved."

"I'm already involved."

Of course she is. We both are.

I stay with her and we look through Ms. Dunn's papers. There's a bunch of stuff with Ron Devlin's name and phone number: his notes to the school board voicing complaints about the humanities class, correspondence between the two of them, meeting appointments, a notice about the cancelation of her class. Letters from an attorney in Minneapolis about a potential lawsuit—Ms. Dunn was trying to get our high school in on a class action case, something having to do with religious discrimination. And worse, information about the city government, like hiring documents, HR records, and a bunch financial papers covered in Post-its with words like *misuse of funds*, *illegal*, and *bribery* written all over them. As Bernie would say, *pretty incriminating stuff.* I wonder if the cops even looked into Devlin after Ms. Dunn's murder, or if he brushed them off.

"Look at this stuff. I don't know, maybe we should talk to Bernie," Riley says.

Now *I'm* the one to backpedal. "Not yet." I put my hands on hers. "Let's wait it out."

RILEY

Apparently my mini-makeover isn't quite enough to hang with the Tori Rollers.

"I don't care what you have going on tonight." Tori puts her hands on my shoulders at the end of the day. "After your rehearsal we're having a makeover party. My house. I will not take no for an answer."

Though it's absolutely the last thing I want to do, and though this makeover session is likely to include more praying away the gay, I give in. I have to get closer to Tori and her dad, and I need to find out if that Degas statue is the one that belonged to Ms. Dunn.

"Okay, okay." I play along.

She claps her hands. "Yay, this is going to be so fun."

"Fun." I pretend to agree.

After rehearsal, Tori's waiting for me in front of the school. She drives an SUV—a shiny blue monstrosity that was waiting for her in the parking lot on her sixteenth birthday. She waves and I jump in.

"Thanks for picking me up," I say, hoping nobody from rehearsal is watching.

The seats in Tori's car are warm, and I don't have to use all my weight to shut the door like I have to in Dez's car.

"Sure," Tori says. "But can you get a ride home? My dad won't let me out after nine."

"No problem." I rack my brain. I can't really tell anyone I need a ride home from Tori Devlin's house. It's not *that* far—I'll just have to run.

We drive past the school toward Main Street and hit a pothole the size of a small car. A loud screech rings from the back as the fender scrapes across the asphalt.

That's going to leave a mark.

"Sometimes I really hate this town," Tori says through gritted teeth. "I'm so tired of everything falling apart."

I bite back a laugh. She has no idea.

Tori weaves through the rest of the potholes like we're in a video game. We only hit two more. Miraculously—though of course it isn't a miracle at all—the closer we get to her house, the better the road conditions are. As we pull into her development, there are no potholes to be found.

"Welcome to Casa de Devlin." Tori smiles and holds the door open to a massive foyer. I walk in and immediately slide my shoes off, worried that I'm going to mess up the perfection. Everything is shiny and new and I feel like I'm in a museum. There's even a marble table in the middle of the room with a huge arrangement of flowers.

"Want a pop or something before we get started?" she asks.

"No, that's okay." I'm not going to risk spilling something in this place.

"Well then, come on up." She heads for the stairs.

"Aren't you going to give me a tour first?" I ask.

I need to get downstairs to look at the statue.

"It's just a house, Riley. Trust me, it's not that exciting. Come on." She pulls me by the arm and hauls me up the grandiose staircase.

I try not to worry. I'll just take it slow and find a way to get down to the rec room when we're done.

Tori's bedroom is almost bigger than the locker room at school, and far more impressive. She has a walk-in closet bigger than my entire room and an adjoining bathroom with a whirlpool tub. It's in the bathroom where we set up shop.

"Okay, Riley, let's see," she says, pushing me into her vanity chair. She sits on a little stool with wheels, like one from a doctor's office. She looks pretty official.

"Your skin is gorgeous," she says, about an inch away from my face. The girl has no sense of personal space. "You're doing the right thing here—just a little translucent powder is all you need. But you do need some definition in your cheeks. Here, go like this." She sucks in her cheeks to strike a sickly-looking-model expression. "I want to see more of your cheek bones."

I do what she says. After all, she *is* in a doctor's chair.

"Hold there, Riley. We need blusher."

Tori holds my hair in one hand, reaches into the toolbox of cosmetics with the other—Mom would be so jealous—and asks, "Powder or cream? Cream." She answers her own question as she takes the little jar, dabs her fingers, and gets busy on my cheeks.

Then she moves on, to work on my lips and eyes and hair.

After what feels like hours, Tori is done. Until I reach my hands up to touch my hair.

"Oh no," she says, grabbing my hands to inspect my nails. "This will not do." She throws down my hand like it's a piece of garbage. "Ew, Riley, ever hear of a mani? We need some Kiss press-ons."

"Fake nails?" I ask, looking at my hands. They did look pretty bad, but *fake nails*? Come on, this isn't the nineties and I'm not going to be in a rap video.

"These aren't your mama's press-ons." Tori laughs. "Look at these beauties with the silver and black crackle design. This is you, Rye. Total rock and roll. And they're short. They won't bug you at all."

Well, I've come this far.

I give her my hand and she peels and sticks. After about five minutes, it's finally time for the big reveal. Tori does a little drum roll and spins me around to the mirror.

I'm shocked by my reflection. After all that time at Tori's hands, I was sure I'd come out looking like a drag queen. But the makeup is soft and subtle. Pretty. My hair hangs in loose waves and the nails really do look badass.

I can't say anything.

"I know, right?" Tori says with a squeeze.

"It's actually awesome," I tell her.

Tori looks pleased. She explains her technique so I can recreate the look on my own. She packs up some supplies for me.

"Oh, the clothes." She looks me over. "We can't forget about the clothes."

"Well, I like your shirt. Where did you get it?"

"You know what?" She tugs at the bottom of her shirt. "It'd look great on you."

She pulls the shirt over her head, exposing her pale pink bra.

And wow, she has an incredible body.

I bite the inside of my cheek. I really am a charity case.

She hands me the shirt and grins. I quickly divert my eyes and try not to think about the fact that Tori Devlin is standing in front of me half naked.

"No," I tell her. "Don't be crazy. You don't have to give me your clothes."

Tori covers herself with a sweatshirt and then hands me another bag. It's stuffed to the top. "Riley, I don't even wear this stuff. There should be enough in here to get you through a week of school."

As she walks me out, I try to come up with a reason to go down to the rec room, but Devlin is in the foyer. He's reading the mail with the world's nastiest scowl on his face.

"Tori."

"Yeah, Dad?" She cowers in front of him.

"Do you know what this is?"

"No." Her voice shakes a little.

"This is college rejection number three for you." He whips the paper in front of her face.

She looks at me and turns bright red.

Devlin's eyes follow hers and eyes me up and down. "Who's this?"

"Riley Frost," Tori says.

"Frost," he ponders. "Your father works at the community college, right?"

I nod.

"Well that's where my daughter is going to end up if she doesn't hit the books. Excuse us, will you?"

He doesn't have to ask me twice. I give Tori a quick wave, slip my shoes on, and I'm out the door. When it closes, the yelling begins.

My heart aches for Tori. *Tori,* of all people. It was the way Devlin looked at her. I've seen that look before. And I've seen the fear on the other side of it.

Tori looked so small that it makes me want to go back in and help her. Just like I wanted to help Dez, all those years ago when his mom's boyfriend got rough with him.

Instead, I freeze. I do the same thing I did with Dez when the yelling began behind closed doors—I chicken out and head for home.

My walk quickly becomes a run.

To this day, I've never asked Dez what happened during that time.

Just like I'm sure I will never ask Tori.

DEZ

FLASHBACK SEQUENCE
EXT. DESMOND AND HIS FATHER RIDING IN THE CAR—DAY

POV shot as seen from young DESMOND'S eyes. We see DESMOND'S hands run across the dash, play with the radio, roll down the window. We see his father as DESMOND looks up at him. His dad smiles and sings to the radio. We see the passing neighborhood through the car window. It's well-kept, with tree-lined streets, families walking, kids riding bikes.

JUMP CUT:

The camera moves to DESMOND'S POV in current time. We see him looking out his car window. It's the same neighborhood, years later. Homes are boarded up, yards are overgrown, rusted-out cars sit in driveways on cement blocks. DESMOND runs his hand over his beat-up dashboard.

JUMP CUT:

Young DESMOND sees an auto parts store out the window as his father pulls the car up. DESMOND walks into the store with his dad.

JUMP CUT:

DESMOND pulls into the same store in current time—now a dingy, worn building.

END FLASHBACK

After rehearsal, I go to the auto parts store. My car smells like a fast food joint and I'm low on fluids. Plus, Mom needs a bunch of stuff for her car. It reminds me of all those mornings with Dad before he left. He was always tinkering with the cars. I must've been about four years old when I started helping him. My stomach turns at the memory.

Inside the store, Mr. Michelson is taking down his campaign signs.

"Hey, Mr. Michelson," I say. "You still have a few weeks to go. Why are you taking down the signs?"

"Oh, Desmond." Mr. Michelson rubs his head. "I've decided to withdraw my name from the race."

"Why?"

We both know he didn't stand a chance—but still, why quit now?

"Mayor Devlin has this thing wrapped up." Mr. Michelson fakes a smile.

"You don't know that, not yet."

"It was my own fault," he mutters, shaking his head. "I should've known." He talks as if to himself, like he's forgotten I'm here. Then he looks up at me and clears his throat. "Now, what can I get for you?"

This news will only add fuel to the fire in Riley's investigation, so I'm not going to be the one to tell her. I give Mr. Michelson a sympathy smile and gather a fuse, coolant, oil, window wiper fluid, and a stack of those tree-shaped air fresheners.

It's still early when I get home, so I hit the garage. Bernie's already in there with Mom's car hood up.

"Great minds," I say, holding up the bottle of oil—identical to the one Bernie just emptied.

"Desmond." Bernie peeks out from behind the hood, his face and hands filthy. "Almost done."

I hate myself that I feel a sense of disappointment that I didn't get to Mom's car first.

It's stupid.

Once Bernie's finished, he comes over to my car and leans under my hood with me as I pour in the coolant. "I got a fuse and wiper fluid too," I tell him.

"You're a good man, Dez," he says, draping an arm around me. "I took care of it, but hey, keep the extra in here. Those things don't go bad."

I nod and close up my hood.

"This one, on the other hand ... " He pats my battered Beemer and laughs.

"Hey, even the Mona Lisa's falling apart," I say, doing my best Tyler Durden impression.

"Let me guess," Bernie says. "*Reservoir Dogs*?"

"*Fight Club*," I correct him, ready to head out.

Bernie props himself up against my car. "Got a sec?" he asks, which is code for *Let's talk*.

Shit, what does he know?

That's where a guilty conscience will take you every time. To paranoia town. I feel my back bead with sweat and I'm sure he's going to bust me for something.

"Ah ... sure, yeah," I say.

"I want you to know that I appreciate the things you do around here. Helping your mom, it's really great."

My guilt melts away. This has nothing to do with my meddling.

"I don't know any other way," I say.

"I know, and I don't think your mom could've done it without you."

"It was just me and Mom for so long, I had to pitch in."

There was no choice.

"I'm here now, Dez." Bernie pats my shoulder. "And I don't mean that in a way that says I want to take your place, or your Dad's place, or any of that. I'm here to help, to put in my third."

"You do help, Bernie. A lot."

I want to tell him more. I want to tell him how nice it is that I never have to worry about Mom anymore, how I like having him around, how things are good now. It's too bad my mouth can't form the words.

"Good," Bernie says, and I'm happy the few words I did give him are enough. "I'm glad. I know you and your mom are like a well-oiled machine, but I want you to take a breather. Stop worrying so much. Dez, this is your senior year and you've been spending way too much time at home. Go out, have fun."

"Wait—you're telling me to go out more?"

It's completely pathetic that he has to tell me to get my lame ass out of the house.

But also . . . it's pretty cool.

"Yes, I know, I can't believe it either. How many parents have to *tell* their kids to go out?"

It rolls off his tongue so easily. I don't think he even realizes what he said, that he thinks of me as his kid.

For some strange reason, that feels good.

The next morning Riley sends me a text that says her dad's driving her to school. She needs more time because of a wardrobe malfunction.

Things, they are a changin'.

I realize that's the understatement of the century when I catch up with Riley during study hall. Normally we get to spend our free period in the film classroom, but Homer wants to make sure we're not letting our other studies fall behind so he insisted we go to study hall this week.

As I walk in, I see Riley. She's sitting alone and staring at the clock.

I freeze.

She doesn't just look good. No, this is something else entirely. Her hair falls in loose waves down her back and her face almost sparkles. She's wearing a little gray dress with tall boots. It's like *girly with attitude* and I can't take my eyes off her. The dress is fitted on top, hugging her in all the right places, and it flows out at her knee. I don't think I've ever seen Riley in a dress, and even though most of her legs are covered, the few inches of skin above her knee has me blowing out every last bit of air in my lungs.

She is off-the-charts model gorgeous.

It's just an act right now, of course, but as Riley says, life imitates art. I'm hoping that's the case, because I definitely like what I see.

I clear my throat and close my mouth, trying to pull it together before taking the seat next to her.

"Hey," I whisper, wondering if I should say something about her new look or play it cool.

Fuck cool.

"So what was the wardrobe malfunction?" I ask. "Because you, my friend, are a work of art today."

"Really?" She scrunches up her nose.

"No lie. What's the occasion?"

"Today is the big scene, and I want to kill it."

"And the wardrobe malfunction?" I ask, trying to keep my mind from roaming in the gutter. I imagine the Janet

Jackson episode where her shirt was ripped open during the Super Bowl.

"These damn things," Riley says as she holds up her hands. Her nails are decorated in black and silver polish.

I usually don't notice things like nail polish or makeup or what have you, but all of this on Riley? I'm starting to see the appeal.

"I could barely get dressed this morning," she grumbles. "Everything took twice as long. Really, Dez, it's such hard work being a girl. I'm exhausted."

She tells me about her morning, acting it all out. By the end, we're both doubled over laughing. Mrs. Moser shoots us a wicked snarl.

We take out our books and folders and pretend to study. But when Riley grabs her book, the black nail from her pointer finger flies off and lands on the floor. Her face turns bright red and she looks at me and groans, "What the hell?"

I start to chuckle. I can't help it.

Riley slams her hands down on the table and pushes herself up to collect the runaway fingernail. As she drags her hands away, another nail pops off. And then another.

Now I'm busting a gut. The look of disgust on her face makes it even more comical.

Flustered, she looks around and begins collecting the fingernail remnants and shoving them into her pocket. I'm laughing and shaking so hard, Riley punches me in the shoulder and Mrs. M. shushes me again.

Sorry, I mouth to Mrs. M. I point to the door. She nods, so Riley and I head out to regain our composure.

"So much for my new look," Riley says as we sit down in the hallway against the lockers. "Who am I trying to kid with all of this, anyway?"

"Well, the nails might not be your thing." I bump her with my shoulder. "But I'd say the rest of it is working pretty damn well."

"Yeah?"

"Yeah. I don't know, though. Those nails are awfully entertaining."

"Glad I could be the source of your entertainment," she says, but now she's laughing too. "Why would people wear these things? I don't get it."

We sit there laughing together until Libby finds us.

"Hey," she says.

"Hi," Riley answers. "What's up?"

"Same ol'," she says to Rye, giving me the cold shoulder. "What about you? You've been MIA the last few days."

"I know, I've been busy with the film and homework and—"

"And shopping, from the looks of it," Libby interrupts. "And hanging with the Rollers. I hear you're going to Tori's Halloween party."

"You know why I'm doing this," Riley says.

"Yes, for your art. I know. It just seems you're enjoying it a little too much."

"Please don't make it harder than it already is, Libby."

"Okay. Then why don't you come with me to the community center on Thursday? It's yoga night, with the instructor you love."

"Uh, no, I can't make it." Riley looks at me. "Dez and I are working on the film. I'm sorry."

I nod, following her lead.

"Oh, okay." Libby clenches her jaw.

I hold my lips tight to keep from smiling. It's nice to be on the inside for a change.

"Maybe next week?" she asks.

"Sure, maybe," Riley says.

"Well, good luck with the film and everything." Libby walks off, tail between her legs.

Once she's gone, I look at Riley, my eyebrows raised. "So, we have plans on Thursday?"

"Yep." She bites one of her black fingernails. "You okay with that?"

She knows she doesn't even have to ask.

RILEY

I feel bad lying to Libby and blowing her off, but I need space to figure things out. It's not like she needs me anyway. She's seeing Jake now.

I manage to pull off the rest of my fake nails between third and fourth period. It's awesome to have the use of my hands again. I might have to agree with Dez, though. Despite the fingernail fiasco, I think the rest of my beauty transformation is working. It's been a quick jump from social death row to new *it* girl. I guess that's what a pardon from the mayor's daughter will get you.

"Hey girl," Caleb says. He circles before landing next to me at our lab table in Biology. "This new?" He touches my shirt.

"Nah, this?" I ask, pulling his slouchy beanie over his eyes.

"Nah," he says, peeking out from under the hat. "You look good today, Riley."

"Thanks." I try not to blush.

Mr. Taylor greets us to let us know it's time for class to begin. It's a lab day, so he writes our assignment on the board and tells us to get to work.

Caleb ignores him and faces me.

"The makeover is impressive." He readjusts his hat.

I set my folder down next to his notebook and meet his eyes.

"It's just a little makeup. For the film."

"Maybe, but it seems like there's something bigger going on with you." Caleb tinkers with the microscope and readies our slides. "There's more to this little *change* of yours. Yeah?"

"Would it be a problem if there was?"

"God, no. Let me tell you, it's working. Especially for you-know-who."

I scrunch up my face, not following.

"Desmond." He sighs.

"What are you talking about, Caleb?"

"Riley, don't tell me you don't know that Dez has it bad for you."

I flush again, but this time I don't just feel it in my face. My entire body is warming.

"I hate when girls pretend to be oblivious," he says.

"So do I—but I don't know what you're talking about with Dez."

"Isn't he the reason for … this?" Caleb's eyes run up the length of my body. "Look, I know you're not the type to flaunt your relationships or whatever."

"I don't have a problem with being open about my relationships," I tell him. "It's just that they've never gone far enough for me to do any flaunting."

"Well, let me tell you, Dez would be into lots of flaunting."

I shake my head.

"Haven't you noticed the way he looks at you?"

Maybe.

"No, I haven't," I answer, hoping he doesn't see through me.

"Why am I not believing you?"

Because I'm lying. Because I'm scared to admit that Dez and I might be more than friends.

"Don't you think that would be *weird*?" I ask, thinking out loud. "Me and Dez?"

"In what way?" Caleb leans in. "Because you're into girls?"

"Yeah, there's that."

Is that or *was* that? I'm still not sure I know.

He laughs. "Hey, people change. You wouldn't be the first, you know."

"I know," I say, remembering Lucas's switcheroo last year.

"This is the time to figure it out, Riley. You don't need to put yourself into a box. Guys, girls? It's all good. And Dez is a good guy."

"He is." I couldn't agree more.

"I'm all for whatever makes people happy. Are you happy, Riley?"

"Getting there," I tell him. "Getting there."

Truth is, I haven't really been happy since that last night with Emma. The night *before* the breakup. It was the last time things felt normal. We'd just gotten done with Tai Chi Night at the community center. I can hear the harp sound effect now, taking me back…

"Oh my God, nice Ninja face," Emma says when we get to her car.

"What? I was into it," I tell her while she flips the ignition and turns the radio on. "I'm really serious with my Tai Chi," I add with a giggle.

"Seriously cute," she says. "Hey, it's a little cramped up here. Mind if we go in the back?"

"Sure," I say. We clumsily climb into the back. She goes first and I follow.

The back seat doesn't give us much more space. It's tight, and since we both have shorts on, our legs are touching—skin to skin.

"Oh, I love this song," Emma says when Tom Petty comes through the speakers, singing, of all things, "Here Comes My Girl."

She moves in and I quickly close the gap. Then she puts her hands on my thighs and whispers, "Kiss me."

It's always a relief to know she feels the same. She wants me in that way. It surprises me every time. I pull her in and her hands move to my waist and we kiss.

Forever.

Or at least until the crowd starts flowing out of the community center into the parking lot. Reluctantly, we both pull away. I ask if she could come over.

"Better not," she says. "My mom."

She doesn't have to elaborate. We've already had many discussions about her situation at home. Emma is so worried about her mom finding out she's gay. "She's frail," Emma says, but she never tells me why.

On my way home, I text Dez. I'm out of my mind, crazy happy.

I can see his light on and I want him to help celebrate my news—I'm officially in love.

Dez never did answer me that night. His light went off right after I sent the text. It didn't matter. Instead, I went to sleep and celebrated in my dreams.

CROSSING THE ENEMY LINE

INT. SCHOOL COMMONS—
MID-SEPTEMBER, SENIOR YEAR—
MORNING

DESMOND sits on a chair and pretends to read a book. His eyes scan the crowd. Once he finds who he's looking for, his body goes rigid.

It's TORI DEVLIN. She stands in the center of a group of girls, laughing. Once the bell rings, they separate and DESMOND makes his move.

DESMOND
(taps TORI'S shoulder when
he catches up with her)
Hey, can I talk to you for a sec?

TORI
(looks at him and beams)
Sure.

The camera moves to a poster announcing the homecoming dance. TORI bites her lip and taps her finger on her book. We can tell she thinks DESMOND is going to ask her to the dance.

They move from the hall into an empty room.

DESMOND
I need your help.

TORI
(looks confused)
Oh?

DESMOND
It's about Riley and Emma.

TORI
(her warm face turns cold)
Of course it is. What is it?

DESMOND
I need you to help me break them up.

FADE OUT

DEZ

I pull into the driveway on Friday, and Riley's already on the porch steps waiting for me. Somehow she's talked me into driving her to Tori's Halloween party. The driving part I have no problem with; it's her hanging out with those lowlifes that has me unsettled.

Rye stands up and my heart stops. She's dressed as Holly Golightly from *Breakfast at Tiffany's.* She's wearing a black dress and long black gloves and her hair is wrapped up just like Audrey Hepburn's, with something sparkly stuck in the top.

Last summer, Riley and I watched classic films almost every night. We'd take turns picking them. I was a fan of Jack Nicholson in *Easy Rider*, *One Flew Over the Cuckoo's Nest*, and *The Shining.* Riley went for the Audrey Hepburn movies like *Roman Holiday*, *My Fair Lady*, and *Breakfast at Tiffany's.*

I get out to open her door. "Well hello, Holly Golightly. Audrey Hepburn, eat your heart out."

"Oh, golly gee," Rye says, doing her best Hepburn impression.

"I still don't like this, you know," I say as we back out of the driveway.

"I know."

"I wish you'd change your mind."

"I have to see what she knows, Dez, and I need to look at the Degas to see if Ms. Dunn's initials are there."

"Well, if you're not careful, I'm going to tell Libby. She would have your ass if she knew what you were doing."

"Yeah, she's not taking this whole thing very well—and I think my excuse is starting to wear thin, especially since we're almost done shooting."

"In this one instance, I agree with her."

"It's for her own good."

I nod in agreement. *Nobody understands that reasoning better than me.*

I pull up to Tori's house.

The large brick colonial is adorned in cobwebs with enormous spiders attached to them. Shadows of people dance in the windows and laughter escapes the door as people make their way inside.

"I'll text you when I'm done," she says, giving me a peck on the cheek on her way out. I pray she knows what she's doing.

Just in case, I pull onto a dark street and change my clothes.

Looks like I need the costume after all.

RILEY

I don't like going back into Tori's house. It's cold and hard and full of the mayor's negative energy.

"Riley." Tori greets me at the door and looks me up and down. "The perfect princess."

"I'm Holly Golightly." I frown. I'm a total fraud—I could never be Audrey Hepburn. I'd be more realistic as Paul Varjak—the guy in love with Holly G.

"Hmm, I don't remember that one." Tori wrinkles her nose.

"From the movie *Breakfast at Tiffany's*?"

"Never heard of it."

"It's Audrey Hepburn's most famous movie. There's even a song about it."

"You and your nerdy old movies, Riley. I'll never understand it."

"I know," I say, rolling my eyes on the inside. "You look great too, by the way."

Tori's clad in a scarlet cape. She's dressed as Red Riding

Hood, but I can't help thinking the Big Bad Wolf would be much more appropriate.

See, I'm not the only fraud here.

"Come on," she says, taking my arm. "We're just getting ready to start the games."

Tori pulls me into the fold. The rest of the Rollers are also in fairytale get-up: Natalie is Little Bo Peep, Paige is Goldilocks, and Alexa is Alice in Wonderland.

I have to say, it's unlike any other party I've been to. Mayor and Mrs. Devlin are out schmoozing with the kids. They're dressed up like that weird farming couple in the American Gothic painting. The mayor is holding a pitchfork, which is very fitting.

Tori stops and grins at me. I think she wants something.

"What?" I ask.

"I need a favor," she says, tugging me into the corner.

"Okay, what is it?"

"I hate to ask this here, but I'm running out of time."

I flip my wrist, telling her to go on.

"I need your testimony. For church?" She looks up at me under her lashes.

I stare at her, pretending not to follow.

"It's when people talk about their life, their path, how they found God. I was hoping you'd share your story. Pastor Al said you could do it next week."

"Wait—you already asked him before talking to me? I don't do well in crowds, Tori."

Next week is too soon. I need more time.

"What are you talking about? You're an actress."

"But this is my real life, and I'm not ready for some public declaration."

"Riley, I need this. I have to help someone with their testimony before I work in the church like my parents do. They're counting on me. Can you do it for me? Please?"

"I don't know," I say.

"Like I said, *act.* Just look at it as another part."

"In church? Isn't that sacrilege or something?"

"You'd be surprised." Tori smirks but her eyes are sad. "Just think about it, okay?"

I nod.

"Let's go back," she says. This time she practically skips when she brings me over to join her friends.

Over the next hour, we play games. We bob for apples—something I didn't know people really did. Well, most of us bob for apples. Tori and Natalie drink punch and watch since they don't want to ruin their makeup. Then it's charades. When it's time for the scavenger hunt, I sneak out.

Down the hall, two zombies—Marcus and John—are pouring what looks to be vodka into their punch. Now *that* is something I'm used to seeing at a party. They laugh and join the crowd.

Then Alexa storms past me into the bathroom with tears in her eyes, and though I need to get downstairs to do my detective work, I can't help but follow. Alexa's at the bottom of the Roller food chain and I know what that's like.

I knock on the door. "Alexa? It's me. Riley."

The door clicks and opens an inch. I slide in.

Alexa is staring at herself in the mirror. A cosmetic bag sits inside the sink.

"Are you okay?" I ask.

She shakes her head and more tears stream down her face.

My insides tighten. Alexa is beautiful, and her tears make her blue eyes even more striking. They remind me of Emma's.

"Tori," she hiccups. "She said I look terrible and told me to do something with myself."

I burn up.

Alexa dabs the rest of her tears with a tissue and powders her face. Then she takes a tube of bright pink lipstick and begins to slide it across her bottom lip.

"No," I say, a little too loud.

I've startled her, and she drops the tube in the sink. I move closer and wipe her lip with another tissue. My stomach is doing full-on somersaults now. I force my hand away from her face and into her makeup bag.

I find what I'm looking for. A tube of gloss. It's amazing that I've become a bit of an expert with this stuff.

"Here." I hand her the tube. "This is better. More natural."

"Yeah, but I don't think that's what Tori had in mind."

"Don't listen to her. You're so pretty, you don't need all that stuff."

Her face relaxes, and when she smiles, I know I have to get out of there.

I ignore my hormones and get my mind back in the game. I pass the zombies in the hallway, a creepy comic book villain lurking in the corner, and two sexy (or slutty, as Tori's been calling them all night) pirates in the kitchen. Then I sneak downstairs to the rec room. Just past the bar is where I saw the statue, that night of the Dirty Deeds. The Degas was sitting on a shelf next to the flat screen.

My fingers tingle. I just *know* it's Ms. Dunn's.

It's dark, so I flip on the light. The statue is still there. I take a quick glance behind me up the stairwell, to be sure nobody's coming. Then I hurry over to the Little Dancer sculpture.

I pick it up and turn it over, but I don't get a chance to look.

"What are you doing down here?" A man's voice jolts me back two feet. He's walking toward me from the other side of the room. Damn big house—there must be two stairways.

I slide the statue back onto the shelf.

The mayor approaches me. "It's Riley, isn't it?"

I clear my throat and slowly release a breath. "Yes, sir. I was just looking for the bathroom."

"Well, you passed two of them to get down here."

"Oh, I—"

He moves even closer. "If you're down here looking for something to spike the punch with, Riley, you won't find it. This is a dry house."

"Mr. Devlin, I wasn't looking for alcohol," I say, having a strange desire to fit into this party, with these people.

"I'm sure." He doesn't buy it. "Why don't you just go up and join the rest of the party."

I do as I'm told. Something about him is more than off.

I text Dez to come pick me up ASAP.

DEZ

Riley somehow got out of the Devlin party unscathed and under the radar. But at school on Monday, her name is all the buzz. Apparently I'm not the only one noticing the changes in Rye. She's almost stopping traffic in the halls.

Yet not everyone is stoked.

Libby charges at me before second period. I can almost feel the target on my head.

What is it with these chick attacks in the hallway?

"Dez, we need to talk," she barks at me, moving to the corner away from lockers and people.

I don't follow.

She waves me over, her face all crinkly, telling me she'll make a scene if I don't do as I'm told.

I slowly walk over.

"Yeah," I say, meeting her eyes. She will not intimidate me.

"I want you to back off Riley," she demands.

"What?"

"Back off, Dez. This film of yours is making her crazy."

"What do you mean?" I ask, remembering my promise to Riley not to say anything to Libby about the video footage.

"The makeover, Tori, boys. I want you to leave her alone. I see what you're doing, Dez. I know you want her, but she's vulnerable right now and I don't want her to do something she'll regret."

"And by something, you mean *me*." I laugh.

"Don't be crude." Libby looks around and lowers her voice. "Riley's confused. Don't tell me you haven't noticed the changes in her."

"Change is good." I lean against the wall and cross my arms.

"This is not good, Dez, not good at all. And I don't want to see her get hurt."

"What's the real reason for this outburst, Libby? Is it because Riley isn't hanging on your every word anymore? Or, because now *she's* the hot one? Which part *exactly* is getting your panties in a bundle?"

"She's confused, Dez. If you were a real friend, you'd see the situation for what it is instead of an opportunity."

"Here we go," I say, taking pleasure watching her blood pressure rise. "You're not worried about Riley. Not really. You're worried that she's going to choose me over you."

"Not everything is about you." She rolls her eyes. "You egomaniac. But I wouldn't expect a guy to understand."

"No, I'm sure you wouldn't."

"Look, I know you had something to do with Emma

breaking up with Riley," she whispers. "I know it and I will find out the truth."

Shit. Where did this come from?

I put on my best poker face and try to keep my voice steady.

Give away nothing.

"Okay, Libby, you're on a roll. What else would you like to add to the list of things that I'm responsible for? World hunger? The Middle East conflict? What else can you blame on me, and where are you going with all of this anyway?"

"Just consider it a friendly warning. I *will* find out what you've been up to, Dez, and I will not let you take Riley away from me."

I hold out my hand, "Well, I guess the only thing I can say is . . . let the best man win."

Of course she doesn't shake my hand. So I slowly walk away, my mind racing, trying to figure out my next move.

"Asshole!" Libby screams to my back.

RILEY

After the Halloween party, I face another dumping. This time by Tori. She comes to my locker between classes.

"I need to talk to you," she says in a low voice. It's odd, because usually she makes a production out of talking—like she's performing in front of an audience.

"Okay," I say.

She dives right in. "Dad said he caught you looking for booze at the party."

"I wasn't looking for booze, Tori." *I was trying to find out if your dad killed Ms. Dunn.*

"My dad asked around, Riley. Marcus told him you were spiking the drinks."

Marcus, that snake. "What? He was the one—"

"I was trying to help you," she says, cutting me off. "Like I need any more grief from my dad. Do you have any idea how he gets?" Her lip trembles and I can't help but feel sorry for her. This is the Tori I haven't really seen before.

"Tori, you have to believe me," I say. "I wouldn't do that.

And I would never do anything to get you in trouble with your parents, either. Do you want me to talk to them?" *I can't lose my connection now.*

"It won't help." Her eyes are watery.

"Don't you believe me?" I ask.

"It doesn't matter what I believe, Riley. I can't have my dad thinking that I'm hanging out with partiers and drug addicts."

"What about the testimony? Don't you need that to graduate from church or whatever?"

Tori blows a deep breath out of her mouth. "Yes, I still need it," she snaps. "I *was* trying to help you, you know. But how do you think all of this looks? Especially to my dad?"

Ah, I knew her whole act was about good PR.

"So that's it? We can't be friends anymore?"

"That's it." She turns her head. "We're done."

"Tori, wait," I call after her as she walks away. But it's too late—she's gone.

Throughout the day, I receive a few farewell snubs from the Rollers. The cold shoulder from Alexa really hurts, but this situation is not nearly as dramatic as my public outing was.

I guess it's more acceptable to be a drunk than a lesbian.

When I catch up with Marcus, he just laughs.

"That was so uncool," I hiss at him during rehearsal.

"Dude, I'm sorry," he says. "But it's not like you and Tori were going to be real friends anyway. You do know that, right?"

"That's not even the point."

"It's exactly the point. It's not like the good mayor would've ever accepted you as Tori's friend. Not like he had a high opinion of you—or *any* opinion of you. Not like with me. He doesn't care what you do, Riley. But if he found out that *I* was drinking, he'd have my ass and then tell my parents. See? I had no choice."

"Yes, I see," I tell him. "I see everything now. Thanks for enlightening me."

I walk away pissed, mostly because I let him make me feel small and insignificant.

I let him win.

Over the rest of the week, I go back to my old ways. I swap out the boots for my old sneakers and my feet are thrilled. I also ditch the curling iron and most of the makeup since I'm no longer required to adhere to the Tori Rollers' dress code. I use the extra primping time and the new space in my social calendar to make sense of the clues Ms. Dunn left for me. But after my botched attempt at gathering evidence in the Devlin house, Dez's enthusiasm for detective work has come and gone. Plus, he's too preoccupied with finishing the film to think about anything else.

I'm on my own.

I start by calling the random phone numbers in Ms. Dunn's papers. Eventually I find the attorney Ms. Dunn hired when joining the class action lawsuit against religious discrimination in the schools.

Things start to look up, until I discover that Ms. Dunn dropped out of the class action two days after she signed with the attorney. After that, I hit dead end after dead end. Thankfully, I've also found no evidence against Libby.

At the end of the week, I'm stuck. So instead of spinning my wheels, I put it all aside for Dez. He wants to show me his progress on the film in the editing suite today. I try to keep up with him as he glides down the hallway. He looks over at me and slows his pace. "I'm sorry. I guess I'm just excited to show you what we've got so far."

"I'm excited to see it," I say, feigning interest. Though I do want to watch, I can't help but see Ms. Dunn's killer at every turn. I just want an end to it all.

At least when I'm with Dez, I feel safe.

We walk by the flat screen that hangs on the wall by the school office—a donation from the Devlins. This is where they display activity information and school news. The red letters that flash on the screen hold me in my place: *All School Meeting Tonight.*

The mayor will be there. I know it. He always has his hands in everything. Maybe we can find out more about his work with the school and his connection to Ms. Dunn. And why she has so much dirt on him.

I grab Dez's hand and get him to stop with me.

He looks down at our hands, smiles, then raises an eyebrow.

I nod to the screen and he sighs.

I try to release his hand, but he won't let go. Then his lips curl up in a smile.

"Rye." He turns me to face him. "I'll go with you to the

meeting so that you can continue your investigation of Devlin. But then will you do something for me?"

"Sure," I say, flushed a little by his intensity. "What?"

"Let me take you out afterwards."

DEZ

INT. EDITING SUITE—DAY

DEZ and RILEY sit in front of the monitor. The camera goes back and forth, taking a close-up of each face. RILEY looks nervous. DEZ beams.

DEZ hits a few keystrokes and RILEY'S face appears on the screen.

I know I was going to wait for Riley to make a move, do the smart thing and all that. But all I could hear in my head was Wyatt Earp in *Tombstone*. He kept asking me over and over, "Are you gonna do something? Or just stand there and bleed?"

Well, I was tired of bleeding and decided it was time for action.

It worked. Riley said yes to my proposal. I can barely contain my excitement as we sit in the small editing suite. It's almost too much to be this close. I want to reach out and touch her.

We sit and watch the first completed section of the film. I have to say it's good. Really good. How could it not be, with Riley's face in every scene?

"Shhh," I say as she giggles at herself onscreen. "This is my favorite part." It's a close-up of Rye.

"Oh my God," she squeals.

"What? You don't like it?" My heart sinks.

"No, it's not that. Your work is amazing, Dez." She shifts in her chair. "I just don't like seeing this much of myself."

"Well, speak for yourself." I lean into her shoulder. "I could watch this ... watch you, all day."

"Stop."

Riley blushes, but I just shake my head.

RILEY

The room is crowded, forcing us to stand in the back. The who's who of our high school are all here. The teachers, the school board superintendent, helicopter parents, and the Devlin family.

I knew he'd show.

Principal Bunker calls the meeting to order and they babble on about dates for this and votes for that. Dez leans against the wall as his eyes begin to droop.

"Wake up," I say under my breath.

He yawns and cracks his neck.

"Okay, next agenda item is our humanities program." Principal Bunker shuffles his papers around the table.

I stand at attention.

"As you know, we'd been considering getting rid of the program *before* the horrible tragedy struck. Before Ms. Dunn."

"We can't get rid of the program," someone yells from the back, which sets off a rumbling in the room.

"I agree," one of the teachers at the table says. "We need to advance the level of education at this school. We can't make any more cuts to our curriculum."

"Hang on," Principal Bunker says. "One at a time."

Devlin raises his hand to speak. He's surrounded by his family. Tori keeps her head down and my stomach sinks, thinking about how Devlin must have punished her because he thought I was boozing at the party. Tori looks like a little girl now, sitting next to her dad and pulling the stuffing out of the ripped chair. Principal Bunker nods to Devlin so he can address the crowd.

"I'm all for advancing the level of education in this school," Mr. Devlin begins. "Humanities is a perfect example of that. And we lost a great teacher this year." He clears his throat. "One of the best. I'm sorry Ms. Dunn isn't here tonight, because we wanted to make this proposal together."

Together? What?

"We were working together last spring to come up with some viable and cost-efficient options to keep the level of education up while keeping costs down."

But, what about the notes? The petitions? The papers?

I think back to exactly what we found. Nothing, really. Was I reading too much into it? I want to find her killer so badly. Am I seeing things that aren't really there?

"We think . . . " He looks down and appears genuinely saddened. "We thought we could delay the elimination of Ms. Dunn's humanities class another year. We were planning on a phased-out approach that would slowly integrate her curriculum into English, science, and art classes. Personally, I was hoping it would buy us time to find a way to keep Ms. Dunn on board. But in any case, she's developed the guidelines that show how her curriculum can fit into the other courses. All we have to do is give it to the teachers and have them implement it."

Homer stands up and joins Mr. Devlin.

What is going on?

"I never thought I'd say this, but the mayor is right," Homer says.

There are a few chuckles from the audience.

"This is the perfect solution to our budgeting problem, and one I know Rachel supported. Not only do I think it's the right thing to do for the school and the students, but it's a great way to honor the work Rachel did here."

I look over at the Devlin family—together as usual. But this time Tori isn't wearing her plastered-on smile. Neither is her mother.

We were working together last spring, Devlin said.

I think about what I've uncovered so far: Ms. Dunn's letters and financial documents; all the papers with Devlin's phone numbers and notes; the Degas; the class action lawsuit dropped.

No.

Were they *together* together?

Ms. Dunn and Devlin?

Ew!

As the praise for Ms. Dunn goes on, Tori's mouth scrunches up, venomous.

Just like it did the next day in school, after Ms. Dunn

was killed. At her father's request, Tori organized a prayer service for the students. Dez and I both went. It felt good to be around people, to mourn together. I think it was the first time I understood why people go to church. The connection they feel. The best part about the service was that it was for students only. People got up and talked about how scared and angry they were. Others told their favorite story about Ms. Dunn. But not everyone took comfort. Marcus almost got into a brawl with some freshmen during Amanda Fisher's heartfelt story because they were too noisy or something. Dez was just as distracting. He was all jittery—bouncing his leg and tapping his hand on his knee. I was happy when he finally decided to leave. It was uncomfortable.

And then there was Tori. She led us in prayer. She read some sort of Bible verse, but I didn't get it. It was about redemption and the forgiveness of sins. Almost like what happened to Ms. Dunn was her own fault. I might not be intimate with the Good Book, but it seemed weird. Surely there was a better passage that Tori could've used. Something a little more apropos?

As I look over at Tori now—her sour face and icy eyes—my Spidey sense kicks in.

"Dez," I whisper. "I think we had the wrong Devlin."

THE FINAL MOMENT

INT. OLD HIGH SCHOOL SUPPLY
ROOM FILLED WITH JUNK—EVENING

The camera cuts to a medium shot of MS. DUNN. She grows increasingly flustered. Her hands shake; her eyes dart around the room; her posture is rigid.

MEDIUM SHOT—MS. DUNN

MS. DUNN continues to pack her box of supplies. She hums now to settle her nerves.

CUE: MUSIC

A film cart holding an old TV and VCR enters the frame. It comes crashing down on MS. DUNN. She falls to the ground, moaning.

The dark figure slowly enters the frame and pushes the cart off MS. DUNN. At first it seems like the dark figure is there to help, but instead...

The person strikes MS. DUNN in the back. We see what the person was concealing. It's a blade of some kind.

MS. DUNN moves and tries to struggle. The dark figure doesn't let up.

After almost a dozen brutal stabs with the blade, MS. DUNN stops fighting.

CUT TO:

CLOSE UP: MS. DUNN
We see MS. DUNN's eyes go blank. But her body continues to jerk back and forth as the attack continues.

FADE OUT

DEZ

Of course, there's no way Tori killed Ms. Dunn. I know that. Little Tori stabbing a woman—a tall woman—dozens of times. I don't think so, but it's not like I can tell Riley this. How would I explain how I know the unpublished details of her murder?

And if she knew the whole story, she'd never forgive me. She'd never give me the chance to explain and all of this would be for nothing. All of it.

I try to hold her to our date after the meeting, but she's caught a new scent and won't give it up.

"So, I was thinking dessert at the Pie Place?" I ask as we get into my car.

"Sure, whatever you want," she says, distracted.

"Don't act so enthused."

"Sorry, but food is the last thing on my mind right now, Dez. Tori may have killed someone. A teacher. Isn't that freaking you out? How can you think about pie at a time like this?"

My mind searches for something to grab onto. Anything.

Surprisingly, I've become pretty damn fast on my feet. I do the only thing I can think of. Throw her off track.

"Because I know it wasn't her," I mumble.

Now I have Riley's attention.

"How?" Her eyes pull together.

My throat tightens. I hate what I have to do, but there's no other choice. "I was with her that night," I lie.

"What?" she yells, trying to mask the hurt I can see on her face.

"Please," I whisper. "Don't make me relive it."

"Oh," she finally says.

This is low. Lower than low.

"It's a long story." I try to salvage the situation. "Nothing happened."

"Hey, it's none of my business." Riley raises her hands.

"Yeah, well, maybe I want it to be your business."

"Dez, don't," she threatens. "Not now." She scoots away from me, closer to her window. "Please, just take me home."

Great—by giving Tori an alibi, I push Rye further away, and all I really want to do is reel her in.

We don't discuss it again.

Thankfully, I think Riley's investigation is finally over.

During the next week, I work to keep Riley close. I find random jobs on the film to busy her mind. Some bogus. Some not. It does the trick, and before I know it we shoot the last scene in the film.

RILEY

"That's a wrap, people." Dez puts down his camera. His smile is contagious. After two months, he finally got his last shot.

We're outside, in the park. I grab my jacket and zip it up. The air is cool and the sun is setting earlier in the day. You can almost smell the frost in the breeze.

Dez waves everyone over and we stand in a little huddle.

"Yeah, now the real work begins," Lucas says, referring to the editing of the film.

"Don't worry. I'll be there the entire time, bro." Dez puts his arm around Lucas.

Wow, he's in a good mood.

Dez turns to the group. "Lucas and I still have a lot of work to do in the cutting room, but I just want to thank everyone for their hard work getting us to this point. Our stars, Riley and Jonah, have been amazing, and the grips and PAs, everyone. It's been stellar. Truly."

He peeks over at me and my stomach tickles. I'm still mad at him, or jealous, or... I don't know what it is, but I'm still something. He gets to me. I don't want to think of Dez with Tori. Like I said, *it's none of my business.* But like he said, *maybe I want it to be your business.*

Maybe I want that too.

"We're only as good as the director," Jonah chimes in. "Let's hear it for our fearless leader."

We all hoot and holler and give it up for Dez. Soon he's surrounded, being showered with praise. I want him to have his moment.

"Nice work, Frost." Stella smiles at me.

"You too," I say. We give each other an awkward hug.

The goose bumps are back, just like I remember . . .

I'm thirteen. All my friends are crushing on the High School Musical guys. I don't get what the big deal is—they do nothing for me. I'm more into Pink and Lady Gaga. But soon it isn't just the Disney boys that capture my friends' thoughts every waking moment. It's the boys on the radio, the boys on TV, the boys at school.

Boys, boys, boys.

We start hanging at the skate park so my friends can gawk at the boys on skateboards. I'm not the least bit interested, until one day two girls come to the park on their own boards. The girls look like me: tomboy clothes, sneakers, messy hair. One girl wears a visor over her mop, the other has a baseball hat on backwards.

I'm in awe.

The next day, I beg my parents for a board.

I start hanging out with the skateboard girls, Heather and Brit, and spend less and less time with my other friends. They're like idols to me. I want to be just like them, especially Heather.

What I didn't realize at the time was that I didn't just want to be like Heather. I wanted to be with her. *With her* with her.

Unfortunately, she moved away before anything happened. Of course, she did kiss me goodbye.

I don't think anything's ever compared.

"I'll take one of those." Dez pulls me from my memories and my clumsy embrace with Stella.

I blush.

"Oh, umm, just celebrating." I move my eyes from Stella to Dez and try to wipe away the goose bumps.

Then I wrap my arms around Dez and give him what he asked for.

THE MAKING OF A FILMMAKER

INT. THE BRANDT HOUSE—
EARLY MORNING

A young DESMOND sits on the couch and watches cartoons. The camera moves in on his face. The 8-year-old boy is shoveling in Cheerios and laughing at SpongeBob SquarePants.

The boy's father, MICHAEL BRANDT, walks into the room. We see him set a duffle bag behind the couch.

DESMOND
(scooting in close to his dad)
Are you going to watch this
one with me? It's a good one.

MICHAEL
(squeezes his eyes shut)
Not today, buddy. I have some work I have to do.

DESMOND
Mom says you haven't worked in three months.

MICHAEL
I know pal, that's what I want to talk to you about. That's why I have to leave today.

DESMOND
Leave where?

MICHAEL
On a little trip.

DESMOND
Can I come?

MICHAEL
Not this time.

DESMOND
When will you be back?

MICHAEL
Soon. But I have something for you. Something I want you to do while I'm gone.

DESMOND
What?

MICHAEL pulls a box from his duffle and hands it to DESMOND.

MICHAEL
Here, it's a video camera. I want you to shoot video of everything I miss while I'm gone. That way when I get back, I'll be all caught up.

MICHAEL shows DESMOND how to use the camera.

DESMOND
(puts the camera down)
But I don't want you to go.

MICHAEL
I have to, Desmond. Sometimes you need to go after what you want no matter what it costs. I love you, buddy.

MICHAEL kisses DESMOND'S head, grabs his bag, and walks toward the door.

DESMOND picks up the camera and tapes him walking way.

RILEY

It's Thursday, the day before the screening, and I don't want to see anyone. This is the first time our school will get to see the films we plan to submit for next weekend's festival. There'll be Dez's film and a few other independents that random students will throw into the ring.

The stress of everything has started to take its toll—not only with the film, but with what I've learned the past few weeks about Ms. Dunn, Dez, Tori, and Libby. All the secrets, lies, omissions. They pile up and weigh me down. I spend the school day hiding out, and soon I find myself heading outside to Ms. Dunn's garden.

I'm not alone.

Will is out there too. He's on his phone, no doubt making some kind of deal. I move to the side of the building and watch him. My mind goes to the video again, of Libby and Will in Ms. Dunn's room that last day.

Once again, Will is doing his dirty work in Ms. Dunn's space. He finishes his call and spits on the ground. Then he takes out his car keys. Before I can stop him, he takes a key and runs it across the memorial plaque.

"Hey!" I run toward the garden. "Stop."

Will kicks the plants and tromps over the mums. He meets my eyes and dares me to do something.

I stop, backing up while he slowly walks out toward his car.

I gather the smashed flowers and leaves and try to salvage them. When it doesn't work, I sit down in the middle of the garden and cry.

Dez knows better than to mess with me, so we're quiet on the drive home from school. I tell him about the garden, and he says, "Sounds like Will."

"Maybe *he* did it." I'm crying as we pull up the driveway.

Dez knows exactly what I'm talking about. "Not this again. I thought you were done playing detective?"

"Who said that?"

"Well, I'd say all of your clues have dried up. Unless you're putting Libby back on the list?"

"I don't think we've totally eliminated anyone yet."

"Rye."

"What?" I snap.

"Just because a lowlife dealer stomped on a few flowers doesn't mean he killed Ms. Dunn. It's reaching, don't you think?"

My head starts to pound. "I'm not sure what to think anymore."

"We have a lot to deal with right now. Can you just put this on the back burner and get some rest?" He leans over me to help push open the jammed passenger door. "I'm saying this as your director now. You need to take it easy."

"Okay," I mutter.

I think he might be right.

It's quickly turning dusk when I get an idea. I run up the stairs, taking them two at a time, to get the skateboard from my bedroom.

I walk into the kitchen, toward the back door, and Dad looks up from his coupon clipping. He sees the board tucked under my arm and raises an eyebrow. "It's been a long time since you've been on that death trap," he says. "Think that's wise?"

"No, but I must."

Dad laughs. "Well, if you must. Don't be gone too long. Mom's picking up tacos for dinner."

"I won't be long," I assure him.

I giggle as I step onto my board. It makes me feel like a kid again. I feel the spinning wheels under me and I want to close my eyes as I coast down the hill. Of course, I can't. I need to maneuver around the uneven pavement, and cars, and kids.

I shift my weight around the corner, the wind burning my eyes.

The angst and anxiety I've been feeling for the last few weeks flow to the back of my mind. Dez is right—I need a break. Everything's going to be okay.

I soar over the road on my board till the darkness falls. Once it does, I stroll back to the house, stopping to look at the last of the autumn leaves along the way.

Though I'm still mad at Dez for not telling me about Tori, I know deep down that it's more than anger at his omission. I'm jealous—painfully so. Then, I think of all the secrets *I've* kept from him. Everything I've left unsaid. I'm no better than he is.

Suddenly I want it all to end. I want to close the distance between us.

I want Dez.

As I get closer to home, I can see him. He's sitting on the stoop, writing.

I skip up the steps to his house and join him. He smiles when I sit down and tuck my legs under his.

We sit.

"We good?" he asks.

I nod and lean into him a little more until Mom's car turns up the drive. I grab his hand and pull him toward my house. "Come on, have dinner with me."

DEZ

Riley took the first step, having me over for tacos with the fam last night, and I'm ready to one-up her. Tonight, the night of the screening, it's time for my big move.

Riley and I share a sandwich as the crowd filters into the auditorium. My nerves are jumping, but it's not about the screening. It's about the box in my back pocket. The one holding the charm necklace I bought for Rye. I've given her gifts before, plenty of them, but I'm hoping this one will mean more.

She saves me the last bite of our sandwich. "Let's do this," she says, leaning in to give me a kiss on the cheek. I turn my head just in time to catch it on my lips—not on purpose, I swear.

Her lips graze mine and my insides are instantly on fire. Her lips are soft. Full. Perfect. It takes every ounce of will power I have not to pull her in for more.

"Oops." She laughs, covering her mouth.

"Hey." I reach out for her arm. "I have something for you." I dig in my pocket and pull out the box.

"What's this?" She holds it in her hands.

"Open it."

She takes off the bow, lifts the lid, and tightens her lips, the way she does when she's trying to keep her emotions from escaping.

"Dez, you didn't have to get me anything."

I watch as her lips curve down. "I *wanted* to," I say, worried that she hates it.

"It's beautiful." She holds up the thin chain with the silver wishbone hanging from it. She reaches out to me and I lean in, wanting to touch her and catch her lips in mine for a real kiss. I brace myself for her touch, knowing I have to hold back.

"All right, guys," Homer interrupts. "Time to get this show started."

Homer pulls me away with the other directors for our introduction to the crowd, but not before I reach out for Rye and whisper, "I already made my wish. Now it's your turn."

After the introductions, we roll the first film and I take my seat next to Riley. The auditorium is packed now, and I'm actually excited for everyone to see our work.

The lights dim and I search for Riley's hand. Once I do, I lace my fingers in hers, happy that she doesn't pull away.

I keep it there for the entire screening.

RILEY

I was five when my parents started taking me to the movies in the city. Our favorite theater is modeled after a Spanish courtyard, complete with balconies and plants and statues. The ceiling even has twinkling stars and floating clouds to give the illusion of being outside. It smells like mildew and burnt popcorn. It's beautiful. My parents used to take me on Classics Night, when they showed everything from *My Fair Lady* and *Casablanca* to *The Wizard of Oz* and Monty Python flicks.

To say I liked it is putting it mildly. Those times are some of my best memories as a kid. *The Wizard of Oz* was my favorite and it's become a tradition for us around the holidays.

I close my eyes and let myself go back to that first time…

Dad gives me my ticket as people begin filing into the theater. I feel like such a grown-up. I watch the people in front of me hand their tickets to the man by the velvet rope, so I do the same. The man hands it back to me with a wink and says, "You watch out for that wicked witch now."

I quickly glance back at Mom, who puts her arm around me and says, "Don't worry, honey. It's all just pretend." She gives the ticket man a dirty look.

We take our seats in the middle of the theater and chat until the lights dim. Then I'm completely engrossed. It's the most amazing thing I've ever seen. I sit there between Mom and Dad and watch as Dorothy makes new friends, meets a good witch, fights with a bad one, goes to the Emerald City, finds the Wizard, is captured by flying monkeys, and melts the Wicked Witch of the West. And all while singing songs.

At the end, Mom and Dad have to drag me out of the theater because I don't want to leave.

As I got older, I wanted to uncover all the mysteries. How did they make the house spin? How did Glinda's bubble fly? How did the Wicked Witch of the West melt?

To Mom's dismay, Dad started telling me about things—the special effects—like the wires that helped suspend things in the air and the trap door and smoke that allowed the characters to magically come and go.

Mom thought Dad was taking the magic away from me. What she didn't understand was it was all magic to me. Whether I knew the tricks or not.

"There's always someone behind the scenes making it

all happen," Dad explained. "Just like the man behind the curtain in Oz."

Dez and I watch our film, both of us content and happy. When the lights come up, Dez takes my hand and leads me to the front of the theater. Jonah and the rest of the cast and crew join us. I warm in the spotlight as everyone turns in our direction … or maybe it's having all my friends so close and hearing the applause. I feel like I could fly.

In that moment, holding hands with Dez with our friends surrounding us, nothing else matters.

The rejection from Emma?

Gone.

Libby's criticism?

Washed away.

The breakups and loneliness and that feeling that I'm not good enough, that I don't belong?

All locked out of this little bubble of happiness and warmth.

Too quickly, we take our bow.

Dez squeezes my hand.

It feels like I can't get enough air into my lungs and I feel the heat inside of me beginning to trickle out. All the emotions I feel refuse to be contained any longer. I let a few tears drop, and I can breathe again.

I feel so … I don't know, loved or something. But now it's not just the show or the crowd. It's the boy next to me, holding my hand.

Something has passed between us tonight. We've crossed over our neat little line. The line that was drawn when I first came out to Dez, when I finally had the courage to tell him I liked girls. It wasn't like he was upset or mad, but I can't describe the look on his face. Disappointment, maybe? I don't know, but ever since then, there's been a wall between us.

After the last film ends and the last crew takes their bows, we leave the auditorium and Dez picks me up and carries me out to the parking lot, laughing like I've never seen before. Not since we were kids, anyway. It fills me up, and I feel a current coming off him.

Dez pulls me into the shadows, and this time when his lips meet mine, it's no accident.

DEZ

CUE THE DANCE NUMBER

Dance montage from (500) DAYS OF SUMMER, SINGIN' IN THE RAIN, BIG, and NAPOLEON DYNAMITE.

VOICEOVER:

DESMOND
The night is perfect and in my mind, I'm dancing. I am Joseph Gordon-Levitt dancing to "You Make My Dreams Come True" in (500) DAYS OF SUMMER. I am Gene Kelly swinging from lamp posts in SINGIN' IN THE RAIN. I'm Tom Hanks playing "Heart and Soul" on that giant keyboard in BIG. I'm Jon Heder in a "Vote for Pedro" shirt dancing onstage in NAPOLEON DYNAMITE. It's the best moment of my life.

I am completely and totally high and out of my mind. Our film, Riley, the night. It's more than I deserve. But I don't care. I'm going to enjoy every second of it.

Riley's smile on the stage knocks me out and I know I'd do anything to hang on to it. After the final film is over and the crew takes their bows, I grab Riley, flip her over my shoulder, and run out the doors. I could run like this forever.

With her.

Or, maybe not.

I suddenly have an immediate need to see her face.

I duck under the awning where it's dark and quiet and I let her down.

I move in so I can see her smile again, but it's gone.

She swallows and stares up at me.

My body goes on autopilot. I have no control as I wrap her in my arms. I tip my head and kiss her. Slowly, gently, I try to hold back a little. I try not to think about how I've lived a lifetime of wanting her.

I stop and look at her. That's when the guilt rises from the pit of my stomach. All the way up my throat. I can taste it.

I have to tell her. I'm going to end this now. I don't want her this way.

"Rye, I need to tell you something."

She laughs and deepens her voice. "He says, breathless."

I smile, because I love when she plays this game and talks in director-speak. She's perfect and this is perfect. How can I ruin it?

Then she looks at me, worried. "What? Am I doing something wrong?"

I shake my head and continue playing her game. "She looks up, pulling him forward."

I move in, kiss her again, and whisper, "You are perfect."

"He says with laughter in his eyes," she answers back.

"I'm serious." I rub her shoulders.

I messed up, I say in my head, because my mouth can't form the words. *I lied to you. I've hurt you.*

"I don't deserve you," I continue.

That is what it really comes down to after all this time.

"Don't." She puts her fingers to my lips.

Then, I know it's too late. I can't tell her now. Not when she might finally want me too.

RILEY

After the crowd finds me and Dez, and the last of the hugs and high-fives have been given, it's time for the after party. We all head toward Caleb's VW camper, and Dez gets pulled ahead.

"Enjoy it now, Riley," Tori says. She's almost jogging to catch up to me and has a fake smile painted on her face.

"Okay, I will. Thanks, Tori," I chirp, knowing what she said was not a compliment.

"It's pretty easy to look good when your only competition are the idiots at school. Wait until the festival."

"And when did you become a film critic?"

"Exactly. If I can tell a film is junk, imagine what the experts will think."

Leave it to Tori to ruin a great night. I try to blow her off but can't help thinking, *what if she's right?*

"Riley," Dez yells from the front of the pack. "Come on."

I look at Tori and decide to let her insults go without a reply. It seems to work, because she just sulks away.

Toward a black SUV.

Will's SUV.

In seconds, I'm back on the case. *I was with Tori that night.* That's what Dez said. But what if that's what she wanted? An alibi. Maybe she had Will do her dirty work. Maybe they're in on it together.

Or, now that I'm out of the picture, maybe Will is going to be her new church project.

Of course, that makes the most sense.

Just let it go, Riley. Dez is right—I have to stop.

I catch up to the crew and we pile into Caleb's camper, jumping around like a pack of wild kids who forgot to take their meds.

Caleb wastes no time as he retrieves his stash from one of the cabinets under the seat and pops the corks off three different bottles of the cheapest champagne you can get at Lee's Liquor.

"To us." He takes a swig out of the bottle and passes it around.

"To us," we echo. We follow suit and drink from the bottle.

Caleb pulls out a stack of to-go cups and he and Dez begin concealing the contraband.

Dez hands me my glass, clinking the top of it with his.

"Uh, wow, Rye." He maneuvers himself next to me on the back bench. "You were amazing. Off the charts good."

Of course I know he's not talking about my performance in the film, so I laugh and play along. "Look who's talking," I tell him. "You could get into any school you want with your skills."

Caleb gives me a knowing glance as he continues in party-host mode. He moves to the table and dumps out a box of eight-track tapes. No lie. Big, black, clunky eight-tracks.

I guess, when in a VW …

"Okay, we have Jim Croce, Simon and Garfunkel, and Tony Orlando and Dawn." He flips through the relics.

"Jim Croce," Dez yells, surprising the rest of us. I couldn't pick out even one of those guys in a lineup.

"I never knew you were a fan of the oldies," I tease.

"Just wait and you'll see," he says. "Rocking back to the seventies is pretty cool."

"Jim Croce?" Caleb asks. "Can do." He leans over the seat and blasts "Bad, Bad Leroy Brown" through the speakers.

Dez stands up, holds the empty champagne bottle for his microphone, and starts singing and shaking his butt. I think it's about the cutest thing I've ever seen. I have no idea how he even knows the words to the song, but it's pretty good.

After the first round of the chorus, Glory and I have it down, so we get behind Dez and sing back-up.

I laugh so hard my stomach hurts.

Caleb moves on to Simon and Garfunkel and we all sit for "Bridge over Troubled Water" and chug our champagne. But by the time "The Sound of Silence" comes on, the crowd is restless and Glory is pretending to slit her wrists, so Caleb puts in Tony Orlando and Dawn. We all stand and rock out to "Knock Three Times," pounding on the roof of the camper until it feels like we might tip it over.

"Shit, guys," Glory interrupts, checking her phone. "We need to move."

I pout.

The thought of our next destination puts a damper on my mood, even though I appreciate the gesture. The owner of Java House offered to host a party for all the film teams the night of the screening, but I don't want to go. Like I have a choice.

Caleb, our faithful host and babysitter, climbs in the driver's seat and pulls out of the lot. He only had a few sips of bubbly, so I'm confident we'll get there in one piece. The rest of us, however... well, no comment. We continue the party in the back while Caleb drives us to the Java House.

Dez and I sit in the corner booth in the VW. He refills my glass with the cheap bubbly. It's sweet and carbonated and calms my nerves—which are out of control. I'm not sure if it's the possibility of seeing Emma or Libby at Java House or the close proximity to Dez. I slam another glass quickly, closing my eyes as the carbonation pricks at my throat.

"Hold on there, miss." Dez stacks his cup in my empty one. "Slow down. Our public is waiting for us, remember?"

Crap, that's right. Why not add my parents to the mix too?

Dez puts his arms around me and I can't tell if it's making things better or worse.

DEZ

"It's just a party, Rye," I say, bumping her hip when we get out of the camper. Within seconds of arriving at the coffee shop, she's gone from laughing and dancing to pacing and biting her nails. She's freaking out, while it's one of the best nights of my existence.

We walk toward the old brick building with the neon orange sign reading *JA HOUSE.* Even though the Java House is one of the more successful businesses in the Heights, it still looks ghetto.

"Yeah, I know," Riley says, running her hand through her hair. Something I hope to do later. "Do I seem tipsy to you?"

I put my hands on her cheeks, tip her head back, and dramatically assess her eyes. I make a funny face, trying to get her to loosen up. "No, you're just fine," I whisper in her ear. She laughs, but I'm not convinced she's okay.

We walk into Java hand-in-hand. It's not unusual for us to act like a couple—holding hands, sitting close and whatnot. Nobody really knows what's going on.

For now, it's our delicious secret.

We walk to the back room, where there are a dozen round tables and a buffet set up special for the event. Riley's hand trembles. She was having a great time before, and now our night is in jeopardy. I can't wait to get her out of here but it's going to be a while yet. I squeeze her hand and will her the strength she needs to get through it.

All the film teams are milling around the parents and teachers. Cameras flicker, bodies collide in embraces, and sounds of congratulations fill the room.

The only person not in motion is Emma.

She gives me a sour feeling in my gut.

I've waited so long for this night. For Riley. I don't plan to let anyone get in our way.

Especially Emma.

She stands waiting by the buffet, her eyes glued to Riley.

I lift Rye's hand and turn her to me. "Time to mingle, babe. Why don't you take the left side of the room and I'll take the right."

She nods. "Good idea. I'll stop by our parents' table first. Look at my mom, she's ready to burst."

I can hear Joan squeal from across the room. That should keep Riley busy for a while. I watch as her parents envelope her in their arms and pull her into the center of their circle of friends. Once she's out of sight, I catch up with Emma.

She starts biting her lip when she sees me approaching.

"Hi there, Emma," I say casually.

"Desmond," she answers back.

"Think it's a good idea to be here lurking in the shadows?" I say under my breath.

"I didn't have a choice, Dez. My boss made me work tonight."

"All right, then can you just work and stop with the puppy dog eyes? Riley's going to see you."

She turns her back on me and stirs the concoction in the buffet pan. "You don't get it." She faces me again and her bottom lip quivers. "You don't know how hard this has been on me." She reaches for my arm.

"I'm sorry, Emma. I really am, but it's time to give it a rest and leave us alone. It's all over now."

Marcus moves between us. I jump a little, not having heard him approach.

"What's over?" he asks.

"Nothing," I say. "Just the filming and first screening. Feels good, doesn't it?" I slap him on the back.

He flashes me a warning with his eyes and puts his arm around Emma. He's possessive and cold. "Yeah, now I have more time for this one." He tips his head to her.

"Yes you do," I say, searching for an excuse to get away. "I'll leave you two to it."

I quickly make an exit and go back to my rounds. The sooner we make our appearances, the sooner Riley and I can leave and be alone.

We spend the next hour mingling and I watch Riley from across the room. She smiles and laughs with people, turning red at their praise. Every now and then, she sneaks a look at me.

Once we all sit down to eat, Homer gives his toast.

"Never have I been so proud of a group of kids." He

clears his throat. "All the films were so well done. So impressive. And in fact, I have an announcement."

The guys give him a verbal drum roll.

"I got a call after the screening. Seems we had some students from the Guthrie program in attendance."

Riley perks up at this announcement.

"They were blown away," Homer continues. "So, Guthrie's decided to send some scouts to the festival next weekend to hold auditions."

"Oh my God," Riley says. She's in a semi-daze. "Guthrie, Dez. Oh. My. God. I'll get to audition before my artistic review. Do you know what that extra face time means? I won't just be a number. Plus, they'll see our film. I'll be a triple threat."

Of course I'm not joining in the enthusiasm. I want Riley with me. In New York.

"That's awesome, Rye," I say, faking it.

Right, fucking awesome …

After the excitement of Homer's announcement wears off, the DJ starts kicking out some dance music. In no time, everyone is out on the floor.

Everyone but me and Riley.

When the music slows, I grab her hand.

She hesitates.

"It's a dance, Rye. Come on, you need a distraction. It's been quite a night."

"Okay." She relaxes, falling into my arms like she belongs there.

We sway to the music but before I can enjoy it, I see Emma reappear. I turn Riley away and pull her a little closer.

"God, this may be the first time I've ever had a real boy-girl dance." She giggles in my ear.

"Nope, remember sixth grade graduation?" I rest my cheek on her head. Her hair smells fruity and is smooth on my skin. "One of the best nights of my life."

She looks up to me. "You want to get out of here?"

"Thought you'd never ask. Should we walk back?"

She nods, and that's the only sign I need.

I grab our coats while Riley says goodbye to her parents. She points over at me and they look. As I give them a hearty wave, I feel a little tap on my shoulder.

I turn around to see a smiling blonde.

"Hello, Desmond Brandt," she says.

My mind goes blank.

Jonah steps around her, with the Spice Girl attached to his side. "Remember Ginger and Nicole?" He gestures with his head.

"Oh, yeah." I muster up interest for my friend's sake, thinking only of getting out the door. "Nice to see you again."

I stay in motion, working my way around the threesome.

"Hey, wait," Jonah says, blocking my escape. "We were thinking about getting out of here. Wanna come over and watch movies or something?"

"No." I answer a little too quickly and see the smiling faces around me deflate. "I mean, I need to take Riley home."

“Her parents are right there.” Jonah points to the Frosts.

“I know, but they’re going out.” I come up with an excuse on the fly—something I’ve become particularly good at. “I already promised them I’d get Rye home.”

“Okay, then, drop her off and come over,” Jonah says.

“I can’t,” I tell him, really on the move now. “Sorry, rain check,” I shout.

“Hey, great film, by the way!” Nicole shouts back. At least I think she does. It’s hard to say because I’m almost to the door.

I laugh, because the old me would never have missed out on an opportunity for an easy hook-up. Something to help take my mind off the secret, psycho crush I had on Riley. A crush nobody knew about, not even Jonah—at least not until a few weeks ago, when Riley brought up Allie and asked why I didn’t go on my date. Jonah knew enough not to ask questions at the time. He gets the bro code. But afterwards, I had to come clean to him.

FLASHBACK SEQUENCE
INT. SCHOOL HALLWAY—AFTERNOON

JONAH
So, who’s this Allie character that Riley seems to know so much about, Dez? You holding out on me? That’s B.S., dude.

DEZ
No, Christ. I’m not holding out on you. There’s no Allie.

JONAH
What the hell was Riley talking about then?

DEZ
I lied.

JONAH
(scrunches up his face)
What? Why?

DEZ
I don't know, it just came out one day. She was going on and on about Emma and I felt like a loser, so I made someone up.

JONAH
That makes no sense. Why would you... oh, oh no. You don't.

DEZ
Don't what?

JONAH
Come on, you have a thing for her? For Riley? But she likes girls.

DEZ
Not anymore.

JONAH
Well, she did, Dez. This is worse than something I'd get mixed up in. You've

got it bad for a gay chick (bi if you're lucky) who also happens to be your next-door neighbor. That's messed up.

DEZ
Yeah, tell me about it.

JONAH
Well, it's not going to work, bud. Even the great and powerful Desmond can't fix this one. Dude, you could have any girl in this school. Whenever we go out, girls throw themselves at you, it's sick.

DEZ
I can't help how I feel, Jonah. Do you think I want to feel this way? About her? I don't, trust me on that.

JONAH
You better find some way to get over it, Dez. This is a disaster waiting to happen.

END FLASHBACK

Well, that disaster hasn't happened. But ever since I came clean with Jonah, I've had to deal with his looks and snide comments and now this—Nicole showing up out of the blue. That's definitely Jonah's handiwork.

Thankfully, I no longer need the distraction.

I practically run out the door with Riley, thinking I actually might be able to do the impossible.

RILEY

While Dez gathers our coats, I make my rounds and say my goodbyes. My parents smother me with hugs and more exclamations of "good job" and "way to go." It'd be annoying if it wasn't so genuine. Sometimes I feel bad that no one else gets to know the joy of my parents. Really. They were meant to have, like, ten kids. When Mom hugs me one last time, I hug her back.

I head to the front to find Dez but Libby finds *me* first.

"Stellar performance in the film, Rye," she says.

"Hey, thanks," I say, with a chill that I can't help. I still can't believe the secret she's keeping from me. "I'm glad you made it." I try to warm up to her. She is, after all, one of my best friends.

"I'd never miss it," she says, looking hurt. "You'd know that if you stopped ditching me."

"I know, I'm sorry," I tell her, and I really mean it. "It's just been so busy with the film and everything else. It's been pretty sucky lately. It hurts just being back here."

"About that." She moves closer to me, lowering her voice. "I know you don't like to talk about it, but I think there was more to it than you think."

"More to what?" I can almost see the wheels turning in her head.

"Your breakup with Emma." Libby puts both hands on my arms, holding me there to listen. "I think you need to ask Dez about it." She tightens her lips. "I see him talking to Emma all the time. Has he told you that?"

"Well, no, it hasn't come up," I say, feeling a fight brewing below the surface. "They have Trig together, you know. I'm sure that's why you've seen them together."

"I don't think so." Libby shakes her head. "They've looked pretty intense when I've seen them in the halls, and I watched them have a similar mini-blowout tonight."

"Emma's here tonight?" I was worried about running into her this whole time. Thankfully I didn't even catch a glimpse.

"Yeah, she's here, but I think she's mostly been in the back. You should really ask Dez about it."

"Libby, that's ridiculous. No, I'm not going to ask him anything. I don't even know what you're saying. That they're together or that they conspired in the breakup? Whatever it is, I don't really care. I'm trying to get over it. Why can't you let me?"

"I want you to get over it, but I also want you to know the truth."

"I think the truth is that you're just freaked out that I'm changing and that I might have a genuine interest in boys. I feel like you want to put me in a box that you understand.

And at this point, I think you'd say almost anything to get me to reconsider."

"That's not it," she says, shaking her head.

"Well, I shouldn't have to remind you that it wasn't Dez that got in the way with me and Emma. Maybe it was Marcus. I hear they're a hot item."

"I don't think so, Rye." She shakes her head, and I walk away.

As I leave, I try not to let Libby's words get to me. That's what she wants. To get in my head. To make me do what she wants: suspect Dez. That was her defense with Reed, too. After he dumped me the summer after sophomore year, Libby said, "I think Dez said something to him." What she forgot to mention was the date she went on with Reed after we broke up. To this day, she still denies it.

I know she cares about me but I think she's more comfortable if I stay in my place as her funny little lesbian sidekick.

Sorry, Lib.

I'm not going to do it.

Not this time.

Dez waits for me by the door, holding out my coat.

I slip my arms inside and move forward with *him*, leaving the rest behind.

DEZ

EXT. THE HEIGHTS—NIGHT

DESMOND and RILEY walk home in silence, stealing looks at each other. They both look nervous.

DESMOND reaches out for RILEY'S hand. The moon is full and lights the way to the Brandts' small backyard. They sit on an old wooden swing. It makes a creaking noise and they laugh. They sway back and forth. DESMOND'S feet are planted firmly on the ground while RILEY'S dangle.

"Do you want another drink?" I ask, trying to find something to break the ice. Mom and Bernie decided to go out on the town after the screening, so we have full access to the bar … or whatever else we want.

"No, I'm champagned out," Riley says. "Why? Do you?"

"No," I say, feeling my palms sweat. I thought this would

be the time to make my move, sure that this is what she wants. Now I really have no idea. "How 'bout a movie?"

I don't wait for an answer. I stand up, grab her hand, and head for the house. "Let's see what's on."

"This is perfect," she says once we're inside. She finds her favorite spot on the couch and nestles in.

I flip through the channels and find *Stand by Me.*

Of course, the book it's based on, *The Body*, is better than the movie, but it's hard to compete with Stephen King. That sick bastard really knows how to tell a story.

I sit next to Riley, pull her legs across my lap, and rub her feet. But she gives me the look, the one that could change the whole night.

"What? You don't like the massage?"

"No. I mean, yes," she says, all flustered. "Dez, don't you think we should talk about what's going on here?"

"What do you think is going on?" I ask. At least I know I'm not crazy. She feels it, too.

"The kiss tonight, the dance, this?" She flicks out her arm toward her legs on my lap.

"Do you not want *this*?" I tickle her feet.

Riley giggles and pulls her legs in, sitting up.

"I just want to be sure," she says, getting all serious. "We both know what *this* means. I think we should talk about it."

"I don't," I blurt out. "Let's *not* talk for once. Let's just do what we want and not think about it. Not tonight."

She sinks deeper into the couch and I go back to her feet.

"Okay, Dez," she says, closing her eyes. "The massage does feel amazing. I guess we can try it your way."

My pulse speeds up; I hope she can't feel it in my hands.

After all this time, it seems too easy. I have a green light to be with the girl I've been dreaming about for years, and suddenly I have cold feet.

The back door opens and we both jump.

"Hi, honey," my mom calls out.

Perfect.

Bernie runs past us and up the stairs, without a word.

"Bernie's not feeling so hot," Mom says when she swings around the corner. "Oh, hi, Riley." She comes over and gives us both a kiss on the head. "Date night cut short."

"That's too bad," Riley says, slowly sliding her legs off my lap.

"What about you two?" Mom asks. "I thought you'd be celebrating with the gang."

"The gang?" Sometimes I don't know where she comes up with this stuff.

Riley elbows me in the ribs. "We did for a while, but then I wimped out," she says. "I'm so tired I can barely talk."

"Let me get out of your way and you two can just relax."

Finally.

"Thanks, Mom."

"Actually, that's okay." Riley stands up. "I'm on my way out." She starts to gather her things.

"Rye, don't go," I almost beg.

"I have to get some rest, Dez." She smiles and then moves in close. "Can we try again tomorrow?"

I nod, trying to hide the disappointment. "How about some Thai food and movies tomorrow night?"

"Deal."

And just like that, she's gone.

RILEY

I take a bath when I get home. My head is spinning and I want everything to slow down. To stop. The water in the tub is extra hot and the lavender bath salts dissolve into steam. I breathe in the sweet smell and slowly sink into the scorching water. First my feet, then my calves, just a little at a time until I get used to it. Once I do, I sit and submerge the rest of my body. I prop my head on Mom's bath pillow and drape a warm washcloth across my face.

I try to clear my head but despite my best efforts, Dez is here with me.

I feel his lips on mine. Strong but somehow still soft.

I've kissed boys before—in plays and our films. And Reed. A quick peck here; an over-dramatic lip lock there. But the way Dez kissed me tonight was completely different. My mind was racing and I wasn't in the moment. It was like I was outside myself watching from above. Analyzing each touch, each movement. Rating it. Comparing it.

It's not like it wasn't nice, because it was. Dez is so strong and handsome. And, he wants me in *that* way. It's so foreign. Exciting, even. Maybe. I'm not sure.

I keep running the scene over and over in my mind, trying to decide if I liked it—kinda like I do with the green tea ice cream at Happy Garden. I always order it and then spend my time testing it, trying to identify the different flavors. Questioning, analyzing. Never really enjoying or savoring it. Yet, I always come back to it. Look forward to it. Kissing Dez was a little like that, and I look forward to more—I'm not sure why.

I ponder and stew and ruminate. I come up with nothing.

Still, the bath does the trick.

I dry off, slip into my fleece PJs, and slide into bed.

I sleep.

Late.

"Hey, sleepyhead." Mom wakes me. She sits on the edge of my bed, her short hair wisps around the happiest of eyes. "How's my star this morn—afternoon?"

"Tired." I yawn. "I feel like I've been run over by a truck."

"Yeah, you looked beat at the party last night. That's why I let you sleep in."

"Thanks."

Mom kisses me. "You were so wonderful last night, honey."

I smile.

"Well, let's get some fuel in you. I made a huge brunch. I invited Dez, Trudy, and Bernie too. They should be here in fifteen."

"'Kay, I'll get dressed." My stomach tightens at *his* name.

Normally, I wouldn't even change out of my PJs for Dez. Now it seems different and I'm not sure I like it.

I pull on some leggings and a flannel and pile my hair on top of my head, holding it together with a pencil from my desk. That's the most he's going to get out of me.

In the kitchen, Dad's working his magic with the waffle press. It smells like bacon and syrup and coffee. Mom slices a ham and motions me to a half-set table. I grab the cloth napkins from the buffet, the ones we use for company, and water goblets (as she calls them) and finish setting the table.

Dez talks to me with his eyes throughout the meal. Dancing glances that tell me he had fun last night. Looks that say he can't wait until tonight. It's nice.

Then, somewhere between draining my coffee cup and cramming another bite of waffle into my overstuffed body, it comes at me. Like a hit-and-run, and I'm overcome with pain—without any warning.

Emma.

I have a sudden and overwhelming feeling of missing her. Wanting her. Feeling alone in this room full of people. People I love, but people who make me feel uncomfortable. I want my friend, my girlfriend.

That's when my heart and head begin a battle. Having gone through it before, my brain recognizes what it is. That regretful aftermath of a breakup. One that can drop in at any time—when you least expect it. One that will, eventually, go away. One, that even though I recognize it for what it is, still hurts like hell.

I need air.

Immediately.

"Are you okay, honey?" Mom notices right way.

Of course she does.

"I think I ate too fast. I need some air." I get up from the table.

"Me too," Dez says. "I'll go with you."

I want to tell him no, but that would seem too weird with our parents staring at us.

I nod and head to the entryway. I put on shoes and grab a sweatshirt, and we go out the side door.

Dez's hand goes to my back. "Are you okay? Looked like you were going to get sick there for a minute."

"I'm fine. I really did eat too much. That and my nerves are still jumping from the screening."

"Shoot. I was hoping you were feeling a little jumpy over me, maybe even excited for tonight."

"Yeah, I'm sure *this*"—I wave my finger between the two of us—"has something to do with it too."

"You're not getting cold feet or freaking out or anything are you?" Dez frowns.

"No, I'm just trying to let it soak in."

"Well, Rye, just so you know, there's no pressure on this end. Let's just see what happens. Dinner tonight. No expectations, okay?"

And just like that, Dez has talked me off the cliff and put a Band-Aid on the gash left by Emma.

He makes everything better.

DEZ

It's times like this that I wish I was more like Jonah. He actually has a purpose and makes a difference and all that feel-good shit.

He gives, and all I do is take.

Trying to kill time before my night with Riley, I decide to help Jonah with his Saturday Meals on Wheels delivery. Though Jonah insists that his parents *make* him deliver food to the elderly every weekend, it's obvious he likes it. Since he's eighteen now, he can do it on his own. Before that, it was a family affair.

Jonah's been doing the Meals on Wheels gig for as long as I can remember. And then there's me, who can't even commit to a job I get paid for. Luckily, I'm a master at landscaping, and the cut from my summer job is easily enough to cover my expenses through the year.

I ride shotgun in Jonah's old truck for his last five stops of the day. The smell of chicken and gravy drifts up from the back.

"So, what was going on with you and Riley last night?" Jonah asks, keeping his eyes on the road.

"I told you, she needed a ride home."

"Mmm hmmm." He sighs. "Do I look like a moron?"

I don't answer.

"Dez, don't be an ass," he says with a laugh. "Seriously, what's going on? Didn't we already talk about this? I mean, you know she's gay, or bi, whatever, right?"

"Oh, you didn't know? I'm so hot, I make gay girls go straight."

"Yeah, right. So what's the deal then? Is she bi?"

"She's Riley, and she can be into whoever she wants."

"As long as it's you."

"Haven't you ever heard of Angelina Jolie or Anna Paquin or Lindsay Lohan?"

They were all into girls at one time and now two of them are married. To. Men.

"Are you sure you want to bring Lindsay Lohan into your argument?"

"It's not an argument. The point is, people change."

"And you're sure she has?"

"Well, I'll find out tonight," I say, staring out the window.

Jonah pulls up to a small brick house.

"Dude, I just don't want to see you get whipped over a girl that you have no chance with. Especially when I know a real live *straight* girl who's interested."

I tune Jonah out. It's pointless to continue with this conversation. He'll never understand, and for once he's looking at me like I'm the pathetic one. I don't like it.

"Are you getting out or what?" I ask.

"Why don't you come in for this one?" Jonah says. "Clara is really sweet and she likes to visit."

"You didn't tell me this was going to be a *Tuesdays with Morrie* afternoon."

"Oh, shut up," he says, taking out a tray of wrapped food. "Come on."

I get out of the truck and the stench of garbage and dog shit smacks me in the face. It's from the house across the street. The house with a bright yellow paper taped to the door, the telltale sign: housing foreclosure. From the looks of it, the people who lived there neglected to pay the garbage man as well. Bags of trash are piled around the garbage bin at the top of the driveway and dog crap covers the yard.

I pinch my nose and turn away. That's when I notice Marcus standing outside of Emma's house, a few doors down. I hadn't even realized we were in her neighborhood. I hold up a hand, but Marcus doesn't notice. He's too busy yelling at Emma. She tries to go back into the house, but Marcus grabs her arm and jerks her forward.

"Stop!" Emma yells at him.

I watch them and know this is wrong. It's not just a typical high-school-relationship tiff.

"Listen to me." Marcus grabs her other arm and holds her in place.

"What the hell?" Jonah stops, noticing the fight.

I don't really care for Emma, but I can't let this go on. "Marcus," I call out, starting to run toward her house. Jonah's on my heels.

Marcus doesn't hear me. He's shaking Emma now. "I mean it," he growls.

"Hey!" I yell. I go up the steps. "What's going on?"

Marcus doesn't take his eyes off Emma.

"Hey." I slap his arms.

He finally notices me and turns his head. He looks dazed.

"Are you okay?" I ask Emma.

She doesn't answer. Marcus releases her arms and she rubs them.

"Oh, hey, boss," Marcus says. "Lovers' quarrel." He flips his hand in Emma's direction. "You know how it is."

"Not really," I tell him. "This is not cool."

"I'm going inside." Emma backs in and quickly slams the door.

Marcus laughs. "It's not how it looks."

The click of the lock on Emma's front door interrupts him, telling us *it's exactly how it looks.*

"Dude, I mean it." I point to his chest. "If I ever see or hear any shit like this again, I'll turn you in to my stepdad myself. After I kick your ass."

"Sorry, man." His body slumps and he walks down the steps. "It won't happen again. I'm not sure what came over me, but I'd never do anything to hurt a girl. Never."

He hangs his head, slowly walks across the street, and gets into his car. Then he proceeds to beat the hell out of the steering wheel.

"That dude has serious issues," Jonah says, peering over my shoulder. "Let's go."

"He's not all there, but I don't think he'll do it again. He seems pretty shaken up. Sometimes these guys just need to get a dose of their own medicine. Like the bullies on the playground. Remember them?"

"Don't remind me."

We start walking back to Miss Clara's.

"I don't know what I would've done without you back then," Jonah says.

"What do you mean, back then?"

He punches my arm. "Come on, we're running late."

He knocks on the door once, and then opens it. "Miss Clara, it's Jonah Herron from Meals on Wheels," he calls out.

From the kitchen, a little gray-haired woman with a walker comes out. "Oh, Jonah. Come in. Come in."

"You know, Miss Clara, you should really keep that front door locked."

"Oh, pitter patter." She slides her walker—with bright orange tennis balls on the ends—into the living room. "It's daytime, Jonah, and this neighborhood is just as safe as on the day I moved in fifty years ago."

"I doubt that," Jonah says.

"So, what do you have for me today, and who is this handsome young man?"

"Chicken and gravy, and this is my friend Desmond." He gestures to me.

"Oh, how nice." She laughs and winks in my direction. "Two gentlemen callers. Well, now we have enough players for Parcheesi."

I raise my eyebrows at Jonah but he ignores me and says, "Sure, we have time before our next stop."

We spend the rest of the afternoon playing board games with Miss Clara, fixing a piece of wood flooring for Mrs. Rose, sitting for a hand of blackjack with Denny, and eating cookies with the Klingles.

It's a good day.

Yet I can't fool myself. I'll never be like Jonah.

To quote *Fight Club*, "Sticking feathers up your butt does not make you a chicken."

Who can argue with that? One good deed will not erase what I've done.

RILEY

With only a week left before the festival, everyone is working around the clock to get everything done. I want my audition for the Guthrie scouts to be perfect, so I head up to school to run through it on the stage.

Dad helped me choose all of my college audition monologues. The selection for Guthrie is from Oscar Wilde's *A Woman of No Importance.* Something that seemed so fitting a few weeks ago.

I'm surprised to find the auditorium buzzing with people, even on a Saturday.

So much for rehearsing.

Still, I don't want to leave. I find a quiet place back with the stage crew and everyone leaves me alone. The crew is moving things and setting up for the festival. I grab a spot and roll into a ball of calm.

Someone sits next to me and puts a hand lightly on my leg. I close my eyes tighter, not wanting to talk to anyone right now.

I lift my head and find Stella.

"Hi, Riley," she says.

"Oh, Stella." It's a pleasant surprise. "Hi."

"Awesome screening last night." She smiles. "Your part in the film kicks ass."

I laugh. Her easy way is contagious.

"Thanks. It was great. Definitely a team effort."

"So, hiding out here for a while?" she asks.

"Yeah, I was hoping to rehearse my monologue for the audition next weekend."

"That's great news about the Guthrie scouts coming. Are you nervous?"

I shrug, not wanting to think about it.

"Well, you're welcome to hang out here anytime," she says. "I can be your bodyguard and keep the public away."

"Thanks, I appreciate it."

"So, have you talked to Libby? I know she was desperately trying to get in touch with you last night."

"She did, but we didn't talk long. How was she when you saw her?"

"She's fine, you know her. She just misses you, Riley."

"I miss her too, but she has to learn that she can't stomp all over my life."

"Yeah, about that. It seems you have a new love?"

"It's not what you think, Stella."

"So, you don't have something going with Dez?"

"Truthfully?"

"Is there any other way?"

"Well, I'm not sure what's going on with Dez yet. I wish I knew. I wish I could be sure."

"Nobody can be completely sure of anything, Riley. We're all just trying to figure it out. You know, I dated boys all my sophomore year before I realized it wasn't working."

Whoa, wait. What?

"Sorry, I'm late to the game here, but did you just tell me you're gay?"

Stella laughs. "Yeah, I guess I did."

How did I not see that coming?

"That must be nice," I say. "To really know."

"I don't know. I'm not too hung up on labels—that's how Tori thinks. She wants everyone in a nice little box so she can decide who is worthy of her time and who isn't. Everything is so black and white to people like that. I just think you like who you like and you love who you love. Simple as that."

Yeah, but what if you can't tell the difference between like and love?

"I guess I just realized that I love girls." She wiggles her eyebrows.

"You make it sound so easy."

"Maybe it is." Stella shrugs. "But I do get what you're going through." She's more serious this time. "I'm here if you ever want to talk."

"Thanks," I say as my head spins. "That helps more than you know."

I spend a few hours at the auditorium, helping Stella and working on my audition. Dez meets me in the driveway when I get home.

"Hey, I was just coming to get you."

I raise my eyebrows at him.

"Dinner, remember?" He sounds a little panicked.

"Yeah, yeah. I know. I just need to clean up a little. See you in an hour?"

"Oh, okay. Yeah, that'll give me time to have the food delivered and stuff. Wontons or cream puffs?"

"Wontons," I tell him before running across the yard.

My talk with Stella has made me feel better about the whole boys-versus-girls situation. I decide I'm ready to be with Dez. I just need a little courage first.

Mom and Dad have another thing at the college tonight, trying to drum up donations. It's been nonstop the past few weeks and I'm starting to miss them. But their absence gives me the opportunity to hit the liquor cabinet. There's not much to choose from: just a little brandy, a bottle of Baileys, a half-bottle of Jameson, and a practically untouched liter of vodka. Of course, there's the wine in the cellar, but that would be too obvious.

I take the vodka and head to the kitchen. In a glass, I make a huge screwdriver. Heavy on the vodka with a splash of OJ. I slam it and make another one. This time not as strong. I've made a pretty big dent in the bottle, so I replenish it with water and put it back in the cabinet.

I bring the drink upstairs and sip on it while I get ready.

I take a quick shower, shave my legs and pits, and stare

into my underwear drawer. Not like I'm ready to go that far, but I want to wear something nice. I can't explain it. I find some pink undies with a little lace—quite a change from my normal Hanes boyshorts—and a bra to match.

After lubing up with Mom's industrial-size generic body lotion, I cover my underwear with my favorite green tunic.

I choose my most comfy jeans from the closet, and have to do a little dance to get into them. My legs are still wet from the lotion and too sticky to slide into my pants easily. I struggle, rolling on my bed, jumping up and down on the floor.

When I finally get my jeans on, I check the clock. I'm running late—it's time to move.

I leave my hair down and run a quick comb through it.

I finish the rest of my drink and brush my teeth for like the third time.

Then, I'm ready to make my way to Dez.

DEZ

INT. THE BRANDT HOUSE—EVENING

DESMOND fusses with candles in the dining room. He lights them and blows them out five times. He paces around the house and runs his hands through his hair.

He goes to the closet and pulls out a blanket. Then, in the living room, he lays it out on the floor.

Giving up on the table and candles, I grab a blanket instead and put it on the floor. We'll have a picnic, not over-the-top but still thoughtful and romantic. I want tonight to be special, but I don't want to ruin it. Riley is getting spooked, I can tell. I told her I wouldn't pressure her and I'll live up to my word. I've come so far. I'm not going to mess it up now.

I put the Pad Thai, spring rolls, and wontons in the oven so they'll stay warm. But who am I kidding? I doubt I'll eat much of anything.

There's a knock on the door and then Riley's voice. "Hey, Dez. It's me."

She joins me in the kitchen. She looks beautiful. I love when she wears her hair down—it looks like silk. As I get closer, I can see that her eyes are glassy.

"Did you get Tru Thai?" She opens the oven. "It smells amazing. I'm starved."

"Nothing but the best for you." I lead her out to the living room.

Once again, I'm having trouble coming up with conversation. I keep busy, bringing out food and drinks, playing host. It's awkward.

"Let's eat," I say, finally sitting down.

Riley does. She attacks the Pad Thai and has a smile on her face that doesn't seem to leave. It relaxes me a little, but I find it a bit odd.

I've seen that look before. The summer after ninth grade, when I stole a twelve-pack from Bernie's stash in the garage. I was freaking out because Mom had just told me that she and Bernie were getting married. I liked Bernie and all, but I was waiting for the other shoe to drop. I knew it was coming—something bad. Like he had another family somewhere or had the IRS after him or was a closet druggie. He couldn't be that perfect. Mom had been close before, and we'd seen all kinds.

Like with most of the important memories of my childhood, Riley was there. Those scenes are always perfectly clear. But as it plays in my brain, it looks like it was filmed with a hand-held camera. Jumpy and chaotic, but very intimate.

FLASHBACK SEQUENCE
EXT. BRANDTS' DRIVEWAY—EVENING

DESMOND puts beer in his backpack, jumps on his bike, and heads off to the caves, a place by the river where kids drink, make out, and basically try to escape. RILEY follows on her skateboard.

RILEY
Dez, wait up. Wait.

CUT TO:

RILEY and DESMOND in the caves together, drinking beer and talking and laughing.

RILEY
(finishes her third beer)
Good things do happen, ya know.

DEZ
(shakes his head)
Maybe for you, Rye.

RILEY
(finishes her fourth beer)
Dez, you just need to believe in the good.

DESMOND and RILEY chum it up like two guys who just got back from the war. They're plastered.

CUT TO:

DESMOND AND RILEY weaving down the road on their bike and skateboard. With the occasional fall and laughing fit, it takes them forever to get home.

END FLASHBACK

Now, Riley's eyes give her away. Drunk and dreamy, just like they were at the caves.

"Rye, were you drinking tonight?"

"Moi? I'm not that kind of girl, Dez." She bats her eyes.

"Mmm hmmm. Maybe you're not plastered like that night at the caves, but I'd say you're happily buzzed right now."

"I know, sorry. I just needed to take the edge off. With the festival and the scouts coming next weekend, I'm a wreck." She chuckles, then proceeds to go into a hysterical laughing fit.

"Well, aren't you Miss Romance," I say, a little pissed. I want her to want me like I want her.

"I'm sorry, but this is crazy, isn't it?" she says. "I mean, come on. Did you ever imagine being here? With me?"

"Well, not really," I admit. I grab her hands, then, feeling them, so soft and small. "But I guess on some level, I've always hoped."

Riley leans over and puts her lips on mine. In an instant, I'm turned on. I really don't care about how we got here or where we're going. All that matters now is that she wants me.

I kiss her back, long and deep, until my brain goes fuzzy.

Then Jonah's questions begin to seep into my head and I start second-guessing myself.

What if she's grossed out by kissing a guy? I'm definitely not soft or small or gentle. What if I'm too rough? What if she'll never like it?

I pull away, and Riley's eyes narrow.

"What is it?" She frowns. "Is something wrong?"

"Shit. No, Rye, no. It's perfect. I just need to catch up a little. Mind if I grab a drink?"

She motions with her hand. "Be my guest."

I look in the cupboard above the fridge, where Mom keeps the booze. Beer won't cut it tonight. The first row is Kahlua, amaretto, and a bunch of other girly mixes, but there in the back, way back, is a bottle of Bacardi.

"Hang on, Riley," I shout out. "I have to get something from the garage." I walk out slowly, letting the cool air calm me down. I search the garage refrigerator for a pop, taking my time.

When I'm finally ready, I mix up a Bacardi Coke, heavy on the rum, and go back to Riley.

She's hunched over, head on the couch, sleeping.

I'm beginning to think it's never going to happen with us. I kneel down beside her. "Riley?" I whisper, pushing her hair off her face.

"Emma?" she slurs.

"No, it's me." I rest my head on the couch while my heart breaks a little.

So much for that.

I go back into the kitchen and dump out my drink. I pick up Riley's shoes and coat, stuff them under one arm, and use the other to throw Rye over my shoulder.

I carry her home.

When I get her in bed, I lean over and pull her shoes off. She has her hands on my shoulders, pulling me to her. I can feel her breath on my face and I want to taste it. Swim in it.

Riley has come to me. I don't even care that she said Emma's name earlier—there are bound to be some scars left after everything that's happened. Even so, I feel that the pieces are finally in place. The stars have aligned and all that crap.

I move to her, and that's when I see it. That *look* again. Fear. That crushing look that tells me it's not going to work. Not this way. Not tonight. That's a line I won't cross.

So, nothing happens. But as I pull away Riley says, "Stay, Dez. Stay."

I do.

On top of her covers.

I'm so pathetic.

RILEY

My throbbing head wakes me. I struggle to open my eyes, and the light shining through my window forces them to close again. I shift to my side and feel my bra strap digging into my skin. I'm still in my clothes and have no idea how I got into bed.

I slip out of my bra, pulling it through the sleeve of my shirt and throwing it on the floor. Then I unbutton my jeans and look around my room, trying to put the pieces of last night's puzzle together.

The clock says ten a.m.

That means I've lost about twelve hours.

On my bedside table, a large tumbler of water calls for me—as well as the bottle of ibuprofen sitting next to it. I take both of them and make an oath that if my head stops pounding, I'll never drink again.

I lay my head back on the pillow and pinch the skin between my thumb and forefinger, putting pressure on the web of flesh. We had an acupuncturist come to the community center one night to talk about the power of pressure points. I try to imagine the pain subsiding, breathing in good feelings and breathing out the bad. Then I try to go back to sleep.

It's no use.

I'm up and I'm miserable.

My mouth starts to water, so I get out of bed and run. On my way into the bathroom, I trip over a small trash can. That's when recollection begins to drip into my brain, drop by drop.

"Rye, I have a bucket by the edge of your bed in case you get sick," Dez said when he tucked me in last night. "It's right here." He took my hand and ran it across the rim of the can, like you would with a blind person. "There's water and aspirin on your table."

My face flushes at the memory. What a child I am. A few drinks and I have to be put to bed. I lean over the toilet but nothing happens. So I move to a sitting position to pee. I sit there awhile, holding my head in my palms.

I slowly get vertical, holding the wall for balance, and shuffle over to the sink.

Drip.

Another memory surfaces.

"*Don't go, Dez. Stay with me.*" I actually said that to him last night. How freaking embarrassing.

The water runs into my hands and I splash my face and scoop the rest into my mouth. I swish it around like mouthwash—I don't think my stomach could take the real thing—and try to get rid of the rancid taste.

Drip.

I remember more.

The. Kiss. With. Dez.

I was all over him.

This time, *he* pulled away. I can see his face.

I bang my head on the wall, trying to shake the image.

When I lean over the toilet this time, I really do throw up.

I crawl back to my bedroom and see a note on the floor. It must have fallen in my rush to get out of bed.

I have to squint to read the scrawl.

It's from Dez.

Riley,

Hope you're feeling better. I wanted to be there when you woke but I didn't think Joan and Ken would appreciate finding me in your bed.

I know this weekend didn't turn out as planned but please don't second guess this. I mean, please don't second guess us.

I promise you, it will be worth the wait.
Yours,
—D

I hug the note to my chest and pull the covers over my head.

The day continues with slow drips of memories. I try to bury them with me under the covers but my phone keeps ringing. Dez and Libby tag-team all morning with interruptions. I manage to put Dez off, but Libby is relentless.

I decide to get it over with and meet up with her at Java.

The bite in the air helps clear my head as I wait for the bus. Libby wanted to pick me up, but I thought it'd be better if we met on neutral ground.

Inside, Libby sits there at our favorite table and I'm shocked; she's always running late and I'm the one who's always waiting on her. I stand in the doorway for a moment, trying to drum up the energy to deal with this latest drama.

Libby looks incredible—as usual—her hair smooth and shiny, her makeup flawless. But something is different. She's staring into space, tapping her fingers on the table, stopping to check her phone every few minutes.

Finally, I move to her and sit.

"Thanks for coming," she says. It's weird. No smart-ass comment, no sarcasm.

"No problem," I tell her, scanning the room for Emma.

"Don't worry, she's not working. I checked."

"Thanks," I say, releasing my breath.

Libby's eyes run across my wrecked body. "Are you sick? You don't look right."

"No, just hung over." I rub my temples.

"Really?"

"Don't ask."

"Okay, I won't," she snaps.

Thank you.

Libby shifts in her seat. "Look, I know you're pissed at me. And I'm not trying to be a jerk. But there's something I have to tell you."

"Fine," I say, just wanting to get it over with. "Shoot."

"Well, it's about Dez."

I drop my head. "Not this again."

"And Emma."

I stop and listen. "Go on," I tell her.

She swallows and then angles toward me. "I found Dez's phone number in Emma's phone. He's been calling her."

"And?"

"Like I tried to tell you yesterday, something is seriously up with them."

Here we go.

"What were you doing with Emma's phone?"

"I saw it at work."

It just keeps getting better.

"You stalked her phone without asking?"

"Well, she won't talk either," Libby huffs, like that makes it okay for her to steal Emma's phone.

"Maybe because there's nothing to talk about."

"Riley, she seems scared and nervous. And it's not just that."

"What else?" My hands wave her forward, telling her to give me all she's got.

"I was with Reed the other day," Libby says, tearing her napkins into tiny pieces.

"Reed? My Reed?"

Or, her Reed.

She nods.

"Where did you find him?" I ask.

"He hangs out at a café downtown."

"This isn't sounding like a chance encounter." I count to ten in my head, trying to keep my cool.

"It wasn't. I tracked him down, Riley."

"Why?"

"Because I have a theory," she says.

"And what's that?"

"Somebody is messing with your love life. Somebody who would have something to gain."

"Okay, no, stop it. You're freaking me out. What do you think this is, some creepy *Fatal Attraction* movie or something?"

"Reed says it was *you* who dumped *him*."

"Well, that's B.S. And you should know, since you went after him. Do you really want to rehash all of this?"

"That's not what happened, I swear," Libby says.

"It's been a while, maybe he forgot how it went down. Or maybe he feels bad for breaking it off like he did. Point is, this doesn't matter."

"I talked to Georgia, too."

Georgia? That tryst was shorter than the one I had with Reed. "Jesus, Libby, this is nuts."

"She told me Dez threatened her."

"Get out."

"I'm serious, Riley."

"No, stop right now. I'm not listening to this anymore.

Dez has been my best friend for years—he'd never do anything to hurt me. He's not the one with secrets, Libby. You are."

That catches her totally off-guard.

"What do you mean?"

"Oh, I think you know. Or should I bring Will into the conversation?" I tighten my arms around my body. I've waited too long to bring this up.

"How'd you find out?" she finally asks.

"Doesn't matter," I say. "Why didn't you tell me you were selling drugs for Will?"

"Sold." She corrects. "Once."

"Then why were you with him, going through Ms. Dunn's desk the day she was killed?"

"How do you know that?" She looks stunned.

"We were taping that day, and you're on the video."

"It's a long story, and Ms. Dunn knew all about it. It was bad judgment, Rye. Much like you're having with Dez right now. I wish Ms. Dunn was here to straighten you out, like she did with me."

"You're going to compare selling drugs to dating Desmond. Really?"

Before I can storm off, some girls from school stop by our table. "Riley, you were awesome the other night in the film. Seriously awesome."

"Thanks," I tell them. "I'm glad you made it."

"I'm taking my boyfriend to the festival next Saturday."

The festival. *The Guthrie scouts*—they'll be here in six days. *Six. Days.*

The girls leave me to Libby. "Ya know, with everything

going on, I can't believe you're doing this to me now," I tell her. "I don't need the stress."

Libby hangs there for a moment with her mouth hanging open until Stella comes over.

"Hi … there," Stella says, sensing the tension.

"Hi, Stella."

Libby's silent.

"Sorry, I didn't mean to interrupt."

"You're not interrupting," I say. "Libby was just getting ready to leave."

DEZ

I ordered the death of my brother…
I killed my mother's son. I killed my father's son.
—Michael Corleone

After Michael Corleone confesses to a priest in *The Godfather Part III*, the priest has a look in his eyes that screams *Oh shit!* He tells Michael that his sins are terrible and it is just that he suffers for them. I wonder what that priest would say to me if I confessed. Is it just that I suffer too? Even though I was so young when it all began? Does my pain count for anything? Do my reasons matter?

After all the fallouts and ups and downs with Mom's boyfriends over the years, I began to realize the power I had in her life. Like Riley, Mom was notorious for picking out the wrong people. I slowly learned that all I really needed to do to get rid of the various tools that came through our door was plant a seed.

I'd make up a story about every new friend of hers that

I didn't like. *This* one was mean to me. *That* one was always talking to a girl on the phone. The *other* one kicked a dog.

I guess I've done the same thing with Riley. Though the whole Reed debacle wasn't premeditated, the rest of them were. When I had the opportunity to intercept a text from Georgia, I knew exactly what I was doing. And when it became apparent that something more than friendship was going on with Emma, I pulled out the big guns.

With Reed, it was easy. It only took a few strategically timed text messages to get rid of him. But when Georgia entered the picture, she was one hundred times worse. For one, she had a boyfriend. Justin. And, two, Justin liked to watch his girl-on-girl porn live. They had all sorts of plans for Riley.

Rye would've been mortified if she'd ever found out, so I couldn't let that happen. I also couldn't let her get anywhere near either one of them. And that required a good old-fashioned threat—with the help of the Heights PD. I hacked into Bernie's computer to get the dirt I needed. It wasn't an empty threat, either. I would've torn Justin apart if he ever got near Riley.

With Emma, it took even more to get rid of her. For that one, I needed to enlist Tori and her bag of nastiness.

It worked.

And now, I guess my suffering is just.

RILEY

"Whoa," Stella says, sliding into Libby's chair. "What did you do to get Libby in such a huff?"

"That girl is losing it. Seriously, losing it."

"Spill it," Stella orders.

"Our Libby seems to think that Dez is responsible for all my breakups." I groan. It's so ridiculous. "Apparently, she found Dez's number in Emma's phone. Then she actually tracked down a few of my exes to ask about me. To find out why we broke up. She thinks Dez is to blame for all of it. She's painted him into this total mental case."

I could've used her investigation skills with Devlin.

Just then I get a shooting pain behind my eyes and I'm sure my head will explode at any minute.

"Riley, you don't look so good."

"I don't feel so good. My hangover is back."

"Oooh, that sucks." Stella gathers our bags and stands up. "Here, come with me." She links her arm in mine and pulls me upright. "Getting rid of hangovers is my specialty. I know the best cure there is."

Stella pulls me out the door and I fall into step with her as we walk down the sidewalk. She has a little bounce in her stride that makes me smile, even in my condition. It's such a happy walk.

I follow her to the diner at the bowling alley a few doors down.

"You've got to be joking, Stella." I hold my head in my hands. "Slamming bowling balls for a hangover?"

She stops to look at me. "We're not here for the bowling. We're here for the food."

We sit at one of the old vinyl booths. I trace the graffiti that's carved into the table with my fingertips.

T.D. loves H.K.

D.T. Rocks!

Ray is a bitch!

I hate James.

J.S. gives good BJs.

I slam the water the waitress sets down. Stella slides hers over to me and I drink that one as well. I watch as Stella plays with the bands around her wrist—I want to get a closer look at them. There are a few bright rubber bands in the middle of layers of thin leather, colored string, and woven yarn bracelets. Some have small charms on them and some are braided together. I wonder what that's all about. Do they mean something? Or is she one of those girls who pretends to be all into Kabbalah?

She catches me. "Sobriety bracelets," she says. "Oh, and a few charity bands."

I feel like a jerk. "I'm sorry. About the sobriety thing.

I mean, sobriety is good, but I didn't know," I stumble. "This is so inappropriate, to expect you to help me with my hangover."

"It's totally appropriate." She giggles. "Listen, I don't judge. Just because I couldn't handle my booze doesn't mean other people can't. And who better to help you over a hangover than an ex-drunk?"

"Oh, Stella." I drop my head on the table.

"Just kidding." She nudges me. "I didn't have it too bad. For me, it was just one party too many and I thought, *this is stupid.* For me, anyway."

I don't know what to say to that, so I study the menu.

Soon a tiny server covered in two sleeves of tattoos asks for our order.

I open my mouth and Stella puts a hand over my menu.

"Let me," she says.

I nod.

"Okay, let's see. I'll have the huevos and OJ and my friend will have a glass of pickle juice and a BCB with fries."

"Got it. I'll get the pickle juice over right away," the server says, patting my hand.

"See, she knows what's up," Stella says.

"Ew, pickle juice? Come on."

"That, along with a bacon cheeseburger, is the cure-all for a hangover, trust me."

I shrug, willing to try anything at this point.

"So, were you celebrating the film's success again last night?" she asks.

"Something like that."

"It really was awesome, Riley. You're so talented. I feel like you're going to do big things."

"I'm not feeling that way now," I say, wrinkling my nose at the pickle juice the waitress sets on the table.

"Here," Stella says, pushing the green liquid forward. "This will help put things into perspective."

I grab the glass. Stella covers my hand with hers and my stomach does a quick flip. "But," she adds, "you have to slam it."

She moves her hand away and I'm left to chug my drink. I close my eyes and open my mouth, letting the liquid flow down my throat. It's sour and pickley and makes my head tingle.

I open my eyes—and recoil.

It's Tori, leaning over our table.

"Just as I thought, girls," Tori says, looking over her shoulder to the Rollers standing in formation behind her. "Riley's back to her old ways. Sometimes prayer isn't enough."

I roll my eyes, too tired for a verbal spar with Tori.

She slaps a few of her dad's election flyers on the table and glares at me.

"Don't forget to vote... ladies," she says on her way out.

I can't wait until the damn election is over.

Before Tori gets to the door, Stella grabs the flyer, cleans her shoe with it, crumples it in a ball, and chucks it at her.

God, I love this girl.

"Are you okay?"

"I am. She doesn't even faze me anymore."

"Good. Now relax and let the potion do its magic." She leans back in the booth and puts her feet up.

I do the same.

"You know, Riley, for someone who's supposed to be embarking on a potential hot and heavy love life, you don't look like you're enjoying it."

"I know," I say, realizing I could use some unbiased advice. "Besides the obvious hangover, I guess I'm just nervous. I mean, after Emma, isn't going out with a guy weird? Does this mean I'm bi, or am I straight now?" I'm ranting. "I don't know what to think."

"There are no rules for this kind of thing, Riley." Stella puts her hand on mine again. I exhale, feeling like I can breathe a little easier. "Don't put yourself in a box. And don't think so much—just do what feels right. "

"What was it like when you were with a boy?" I ask, hoping I'm not prying too much. "I mean, I didn't get very far in my previous relationships."

"Well." She laughs. "Once you can get past what they're packing down there, it's really not *that* different."

Just then, the waitress drops the burger on the table. I can feel my face turning bright red.

How embarrassing. She must've heard everything.

Stella and I stare at the pile of meat in front of us. Then Stella shrugs her shoulders and I crack up.

"Oh, God, I can't even go there right now," I say, struggling for air.

"You don't have to," she says when we're finally able

to calm down. "Just listen to your heart, Riley. I know it sounds cheesy, but really listen. It won't steer you wrong."

She pushes my burger over. "Now, eat."

The high from the weekend is over and school drags on Monday. During third period, I skip Geometry. I can't face Libby. Or, I don't want to—which I'm sure is making her feel even more superior than she already does. But I don't care about that either.

On the way to the auditorium, I have to pass Ms. Dunn's old classroom. Mrs. Craig is now using it for Statistics. I can't stand the thought of somebody else using her things so I run by the room, keeping my eyes straight ahead.

Once I get to the stairwell, I see Emma.

"Riley." She smiles, just the way she used to.

"Hi," I say, trying to sound uninterested even though every cell in my body is on high alert.

Her face deflates a little but her eyes search mine when she asks, "How've you been?"

"Busy." I shuffle my feet, willing them to hold still. "You know, the film and all."

"Yeah. You were really great, Riley. Amazing."

"You came to the screening?" I clear my throat, trying to mask my excitement.

"I was there, just to see your film. Viv wouldn't let me off for the entire screening. She was so freaked out about the after party—it was an all-hands-on-deck situation."

"Wow, I'm ah . . . that's cool. Thanks for the support."

"I wouldn't have missed it," she says. And then, as quickly as the wall came down, it goes back up and she looks past me.

"Hello, ladies." Dez comes up behind me. "What, are you cutting class?" He pokes at my ribs. "Hey Emma, what's up?"

"I was just leaving," Emma says, and she leaves so fast I don't get a chance to say goodbye.

"So, what's up there?" Dez asks, a little too intense for comfort. Libby's accusations seep into my head as I look at him—I'm furious that she has me second-guessing him.

"Nothing. I ran into her on my way to the auditorium," I tell him, shaking off my skepticism. "I'm not feeling Geometry today, so I thought I'd come down here and block a few things for my audition."

"You'll be perfect, Riley."

"No, I still need some work. I really want to be at the top of my game for the Guthrie scouts."

"You're going to be great."

The way he says it makes me almost believe it.

"Will I see you later?" he asks.

I nod, and Dez leans in for a quick peck. But once his lips touch mine, I quickly move back.

He looks at me, resting his hands on my shoulders. "Is that not okay?"

"No," I stutter. "I mean, yeah—I don't . . . I don't know. I'm not into the whole PDA thing."

"There's nobody here. I wouldn't do that to you."

"I know. I'm sorry. I'm just nervous about the auditions and seeing Emma. It's just been a weird day."

"You don't still have feelings for her, do you?" He looks pained when he asks.

"No, it's not that. I don't know—I just get the feeling that she's not telling me something."

"Rye, when things end, they usually end badly. It's just the way it is. Otherwise they wouldn't end. You deserve a fresh start."

I know he's right. And I want him to be part of that fresh start.

DEZ

Riley moves closer to me and I don't hesitate. I meet her halfway—probably more than half. Her lips part and mine lock on hers. She smells like cherries and tastes sweet. I close my eyes, this time not worrying about my performance or my guilt or anything. Instead, I pour a lifetime of wanting her, loving her, into the kiss. There's so much intensity that I feel it in my bones. I glide my fingers along her skin, her hair... and then, wrapping my arms around her, I hold us there in that moment.

"How's that for a fresh start," she whispers into my mouth.

I answer her with another kiss. This time, slow and deep, and not quite as gentle.

"I like your thinking, Frost," I say when I finally unlock my lips from hers. My arms still hold her tight like I'm afraid she's going to run away. I guess in some ways, I am.

"So, this is what it feels like?" she asks.

"To, what—be with a guy?" I ask, not liking the direction our conversation is taking.

"No, to be wanted."

"You have no idea," I whisper in her ear, burying my head in her hair.

But we're no longer alone. Someone clears their throat, but I keep my eyes on Riley.

"All right, Mr. Brandt, let's break it up there," Mr. Green says with a tap on my shoulder.

Riley leaps out of my arms before I have a chance to answer him.

"Move along now," he says, shooing us away.

I grab Riley's hand and walk her to the auditorium.

RILEY

It's hard to concentrate after that kiss, but after Dez heads back to class, I try working through my monologue.

As I mark my way through, I feel a presence. Then I hear a loud thud.

"Sorry," I hear a girl's voice call out. She comes out from behind the curtain. It's Stella.

"Hi, sorry," she says again. "I didn't mean to interrupt."

"It's okay. I'm just avoiding Geometry and stressing over the audition."

"That's right. The Guthrie posse."

"Yep, and I'm crazed." I walk over to her, comforted to be talking to someone who isn't involved in all the drama in my life. "So, what are you doing?"

"Just getting this place ready for the festival and fixing some of the props for the auditions," she says.

"Ah, you must be the man behind the curtain."

"What's that now?" she asks, confused.

"Like in *The Wizard of Oz*?"

"No, that ain't me. I'm just the chick who fixes broken stuff."

And then it strikes me just how pretty Stella is. Maybe that's what love or lust—or whatever's going on with me and Dez—does to people. Makes everyone look better, brighter.

"Ya know, you look more like the chick who should be *on* stage."

"No, no way." Stella looks around. "I like it back here. In the shadows. Working on the film was great, but I like being in the theater. This place has so many hidden mysteries, know what I mean? All the ghosts. And you never know what you'll find in the rafters."

"I get it. That's actually the part I like most about acting. You think you know a person, a character, but you never do. You have to pull them back, layer by layer—like an onion—to uncover the mystery. To really find out what's going on."

"Exactly."

"So, I never really said thanks yesterday for the hangover remedy."

"My pleasure. Just don't make a habit of it, okay?"

"Yeah, I think my drinking days are over for a while."

"I'm glad to hear it. And you've figured things out with Dez?"

"You know, I think I finally have," I tell her, still feeling the heat from his kiss.

DEZ

On Wednesday morning, I walk Riley to her locker. Her eyes narrow as she takes in the sight. Red, white, and blue streamers hang from her locker door, along with a huge picture of Mayor Devlin.

Looks like Tori is rubbing it in.

Of course we're not surprised Devlin won the election. With Michelson pulling out, the only other competition was some no-name twenty-five-year-old.

Still, it hurts.

"Well, there goes the town," Riley says, trying to be upbeat.

This is the last thing she needs. With the festival coming up in just a few days, she's been on edge and I can tell she hasn't been sleeping. Her eyes are puffy and dull.

Doesn't matter. She's still beautiful.

"Think of it this way," I say. "It's not like the Heights can get any worse."

I help Rye pull off the streamers and then pull her in for a kiss.

She doesn't pull back.

"Another switcheroo, huh, Riley?" Tori stops by to admire her handiwork. "Back to boys again?"

Rye and I flip Tori off in unison and resume our kiss.

I don't even care if I have to suffer Tori's wrath later. I've come too close now to let anything get in my way with Rye.

I won't.

When the day of the festival finally arrives, I can't do anything but pace around my bedroom. Every muscle in my body aches. I'm wound so tight, and I'm afraid the smallest thing might cause me to unravel. *Just one more time*, I keep telling myself. I just have to interfere one more time. Otherwise we'll never stand a chance. After tonight, though, that's it. Then Riley and I will make it on our own. No more lies or games or tricks.

Riley has made her decision. That much was clear on Monday. I've been replaying the kiss all week. *How's that for a fresh start*, she said. My hormones kick into overdrive thinking about her voice. Her body. The kiss.

I don't want to do this, but I see no other way. I slip on my sweatshirt and look out my window. It looks like Riley's bedroom light is on.

It's safe to leave.

I gather my supplies, throw my camera bag around my back, and sneak out the back door. As far as Riley knows, I'm home preparing for the festival. I bring my camera with me as an alibi, just in case.

Once I'm out on the street, I see a car moving really slowly—like someone is looking for a street address. I jump behind some bushes and wait for it to pass. As the car reaches the light, I can see the driver.

My heart starts pounding.

It's Marcus.

He didn't see me. He didn't see me.

I try to settle my breathing but can't. That's it, I'm calling it off. I can't do this. Yet my body doesn't stop. It's like I'm watching myself from behind the camera lens as I work up to a jog.

I make it to the school and go to the side door. I flip my hood up and walk through the empty hallway to the theater on the west side.

Once I make it into the auditorium, I set my camera down. I have forty minutes before anyone is expected. I checked the crew's schedule.

The place is dark, so I grab my flashlight and scissors and head straight to the dressing rooms. I shine the light on the floor and weave around the props and equipment. I enter the door that says *Ladies*.

It smells like perfume and baby powder inside. I hold the knob and shut the door, trying not to make a sound.

I use my flashlight to get my bearings in the room, finding a bunch of garment bags hanging in the corner. I flip through them until I come to one labeled *Riley.*

I take it down from the rack and lay it on the floor, inching the zipper open. It releases a sweet cherry smell. *Riley.* I reach in and slowly pull each item out.

I run my hands over her clothes and ache, thinking about how she modeled this outfit for me. She always wants my opinion.

How have things gotten so far out of my control?

How could I possibly do this to Rye?

If only there was another way.

Scissors in hand, I gently cut and tear the stitching on the fabric, trying not to make it too obvious.

My heart races and all I can hear in my head is Chris Isaak's twangy guitar and his low voice singing "Baby Did a Bad Bad Thing."

Like I said, it's the soundtrack for the B-movie that's become my life.

After all the ripping and tearing is complete, I wipe my forehead and tuck everything back inside the bag.

I hang the bag back into its original spot and find the cubby holding all the shoes.

I take Riley's boots out and reach in my pack for a hammer. I use it to pry out a nail from the heel of the shoe. I stuff the nail into my pocket and work on the second one.

That's when I hear it.

Voices.

I flick off the switch on my flashlight, blinded in the darkness.

The voices get closer.

I feel around for the cubby and shove the boots back in.

Then I wiggle toward the dressing table, tucking my body into a ball underneath.

I close my eyes and hold my breath.

RILEY

In my room, I hear a honk outside. Stella is waiting in her car. We don't have a lot of time, so I run out to meet her.

I asked her to take me to the auditorium this afternoon. I don't want Dez, or anyone else, to know how nervous I am. So I plan to just do one more run-through before everyone starts arriving for the festival.

Plus, Stella's into visualization and positive energy and all that, and she has some exercises to help me prepare for tonight.

The auditorium is empty. Each step we take echoes throughout the room. It's a little eerie.

Stella goes behind the curtain and flips the lights on low.

I walk out to center stage and begin marking my positions and saying the words in my head.

I'm sweating with nerves.

After I mark it a few more times, I feel ready.

I stand on stage and look off to the side where Stella sits. "Now what?" I ask.

She gets up and struts over in her happy walk, settling behind me. "There's no right or wrong way, Riley. Just look out into the audience. Imagine success, imagine joy, imagine that you are entertaining them—making them happy, sharing your gift."

I look back at her. "Really?"

"I'm serious, it works."

Stella leaves me to it and for the next several minutes, I visualize and meditate and send all my good and karmic energy onto the stage.

I do feel a little better.

As I get ready to start Mrs. Allonby's funny monologue from *A Woman of No Importance*, my mind flashes to Ms. Dunn. She loved Oscar Wilde, and loved this play for its feminism.

I channel her strength as I begin.

"*The Ideal Man.*" I bellow the first line, strutting downstage. "*Oh, the Ideal Man should talk to us as if we were goddesses, and treat us as if we were children. He should refuse all our serious requests, and gratify every one of our whims. He should encourage us to have caprices, and forbid us to have missions.*"

I continue on, getting through the entire thing without stumbling. I deadpan and exaggerate in all the right places.

When Stella returns, I'm pretty happy with my performance.

She points to her phone. "Time to go. People will be here soon and you need to get home."

"Yeah, I'm good now," I tell her. "Thanks for this."

"Anytime," she says, leading me off the stage.

DEZ

INT. HIGH SCHOOL AUDITORIUM
DRESSING ROOM—AFTERNOON

The camera moves in on a bead of sweat flowing down DESMOND'S face. He's crouched under a table in the dressing room. He looks at his watch. We hear the ticking of time. Ten minutes pass. Then fifteen.

I crawl out from under the dressing table and plan my getaway. I sneak out of the room and watch as the light goes out and the backstage door closes.

I stretch out the kink in my neck and take a deep breath. *That was so close.*

When I'm done messing with Riley's audition clothes, I hide the evidence in my pack and sling my camera bag over my shoulder.

But then I'm paralyzed by a flood of white light. I can't

see a thing. I cover my eyes until they adjust. There's a glow on stage and multiple spotlights, making small circles appear across the floor.

A pair of black sneakers steps into one of them.

"What are you doing, Dez?"

My mouth goes dry.

It's Stella.

I slow my breathing and try to relax. I've had so much practice that it's not that hard to do.

"Riley lost her charm necklace," I say. "I needed to grab some stuff anyway, so I told her I'd look for it." I wave my flashlight as proof.

"Oh, she didn't mention that." Stella pulls her brows together.

Why would she mention it to you?

"Yeah, she's pretty stressed about tonight," I add, to cover my tracks.

"Do you want some help?" Stella asks.

"No, that's okay. It's a long shot. I've retraced all her steps and can't find it. I'm going to go over them one more time."

"Okay. I'll be in the wings if you need me. I'll keep my eyes out for it," Stella says. "See you in a bit."

"Yeah, see ya," I say.

I pretend to search for the mystery necklace a little longer before running out the back.

I have just minutes to get home.

I sprint the whole way.

RILEY

Dez is running late, so Mom drives me to the school. She's quiet, keeps the radio on low, and taps on the steering wheel. She might be more nervous than I am.

"I'll be cheering you on in spirit, sweetie," she says when she stops at the front door. She brings me in for a tight hug and kiss on the head. "I wish we didn't have this thing for Dad tonight, but we can't miss it. If I'd known about Guthrie coming..."

"Mom." I gently pull away. "It's okay. I might do better without a crowd." I smile. "Plus, I have Dez. It'll be just fine."

In the halls, I try to shake off my nerves. I hear footsteps behind me. Thinking it's one of the crew, I turn around, wanting the distraction.

Instead, I almost slam into Will. His eyes are just as icy as they were that day in the garden. My hands go cold, and I quickly turn back around and pick up my pace.

"Wait, Riley," he calls out.

I keep moving.

"Hey, I want to talk to you about that video."

Oh no.

I turn the corner.

"Libby told me what you saw," he yells.

It's him. He did it. He wants to shut me up.

I get closer to the auditorium and there are people everywhere. I blend into the crowd and keep moving.

Once I make it to the auditorium, I'm shaking. I feel like I'm losing it. I don't know what to think about Will or Tori or Devlin or even Libby. I feel like I can't trust my instincts anymore.

I try to push it all away for now. Thankfully, I fit right into the chaos. You can actually *feel* the tension in the air. It's much worse than it was at our screening. Homer is so frazzled that he makes me look calm. People from eight Midwest schools are preparing for auditions and interviews with local community colleges, tech schools, and a few universities. The Guthrie program gets to use the main auditorium before the film screenings begin. The staff tries to keep the auditions private but people are sneaking in, in clusters.

My audition is right in the middle of the line-up. Dez gave out the times for our group last week.

I keep looking over my shoulder, worried that Will's going to come for me. I hang out and wait for Dez to arrive with our sandwich, but he never does. I'm still in my sweats, but don't want to go to the dressing room until I see Dez. Instead, it's Stella who joins me.

"Are you ready for tonight?"

"As I'll ever be, I guess." I take my shirt sleeve and dab the sweat beads forming on my forehead.

"Hey, are you okay?"

I shake my head, knowing Stella will set me straight.

"What is it?"

"Okay, don't think I'm crazy."

"Too late." She pats my hand.

"I think Will is up to something. Something bad."

"Will Thomas?"

"Yeah. I think he may have hurt Ms. Dunn."

"What do you mean, *hurt*?"

"I think he's the one who killed her," I blurt out.

"*Think?*"

"Yes, it's just a theory right now," I say, and then it comes to me. "Hey, could you do me a favor?"

"I think so. What is it?"

"Do they still give the office workers keys?"

"Yeah, but just for the reception area. Not the principal's office or anything."

"Where do they keep attendance records?"

Stella grins. "I can access them from the computer in the reception area. What do you need to know?"

"Will's attendance record in September."

"Done," she says. "But I have one question for you."

"Okay."

"Just how many *theories* do you have about Ms. Dunn's murder?"

"About four. Maybe five," I admit, feeling my credibility slip.

Stella's demeanor doesn't change. She just nods and looks at her watch. "All right, Riley. But enough of this for right now. You need to get in your happy place for the audition."

"You're right." I close my eyes and take a few deep breaths. I feel better knowing Stella is on the case with me.

"I have something for you," she says, reaching for my hand. She drops one of her bracelets in my palm. "It's for luck."

"Cool, thanks," I say, touched.

"Knock 'em dead, Riley."

I clench the bracelet in my hand and smile.

She stops before heading to the back. "Oh, by the way, did Dez find your necklace?"

"Necklace?"

"Yeah. He was here earlier looking for it. Did he find it?"

Before I can answer, Homer interrupts us.

"Riley, I need you over here for a minute."

I run through my monologue with Homer, but I can't concentrate. Dez is still a no-show.

"He'll be here, Riley," Homer says. "Let's just get you through your scene."

He works with me in a small room down the hall from the auditorium. I wait until the last possible minute to get dressed. I picked out a tasteful white blouse and black pants, and I don't want to stain it with the sweat that's been secreting from my body for the last hour.

When I can't wait any longer, I go to the dressing room. There's still no sign of Dez.

DEZ

By the time I get to the auditorium, people are starting to file in. Homer grabs me like I'm his long lost son. Then he shakes me when he realizes that I'm okay.

"I don't even want to know," he snaps before pushing me toward the auditorium.

Moments later, I sit with the others and watch the auditions.

Except, unlike the others, *I* wait.

For disaster.

RILEY

In the dressing room, I put on my clothes while trying to do the breathing exercises Stella taught me. I must be in the zone because I don't hear any of the commotion until Stella's face is directly in front of mine.

"Where've you been?" she screams.

DEZ

INT. HIGH SCHOOL AUDITORIUM—EVENING

Slow motion—Riley on stage

RILEY is shaky when she comes out on stage. Each step is labored. The camera tightens on parts of her body: her chest heaving; her hands fidgeting; her eyes darting around the room.

DESMOND grips his chair so tight, his knuckles turn white.

Riley's not at the top of her game like she wanted to be, but so far, I might be the only one to notice. She finds my face in the audience and gives me a questioning glance. *Where were you?* she asks with her eyes.

I look away.

Forget the butterflies; I have ugly, angry crows flapping

away in my gut. Chewing on my insides trying to escape. I'm afraid for Riley.

Suddenly, I want to stop the audition. I want to take back everything I've done. What was I thinking? I am the world's biggest asshole.

I wipe my sweaty hands on my pants. It's too late to do anything.

The spotlight shines on Riley.

"*The Idle Man*," she says, then immediately looks down. That's when I notice her first slip. She got the line wrong. She catches herself and tries again. "*The* Ideal *Man*," she says in a small voice. It's not enough for anyone in the audience to really notice, but there's no doubt the Guthrie scout caught the mistake. Plus, he's already pissed she was late.

At this point, Riley's supposed to strut downstage, but her strut looks more like a limp.

I'm so nervous, I might pass out.

"*Oh, the Ideal Man should talk to us as if we were goddesses, and treat us as if we were children.*" She continues the monologue, but she's only going through the motions. Her voice is flat; there's no emotion.

And then, as she moves, her clothes literally start coming apart at the seams. She walks around the stage slowly and clumsily, like she's bracing for a fall. She struggles to keep going.

It's uncomfortable to watch.

When I see her wrestle with her pants and boot, I have to look away. There's a gap in the waistband of her pants and she's trying to keep them up with alternating hands. Meanwhile, the heel on her boot is bent, hanging on by one skinny nail.

People are frozen, watching. Stella has come out to the audience, and her face is one of horror. I act concerned as people give me looks, but all I'm thinking about is the greater good: Riley's future perfect audition for Tisch and our lives in New York City—as they are meant to be. Someday the two of us will laugh about this night.

It's the only thing that keeps me going.

RILEY

It's a long walk of shame out of the audition. I get a few pats on the back, a ton of stares, and a smirk from Tori. She tells me *told ya so* with her eyes. I sneak into a quiet classroom to hide. I have thirty minutes before the screenings start.

I just don't understand how so many things could go wrong in one audition.

Well, Guthrie is out of the picture now, but there might still be a chance with the other schools.

I wish Ms. Dunn was here. She'd know what to do.

I'm such an idiot. This is what got me into this position in the first place. My obsession with Ms. Dunn and playing detective like I could make a difference. It's been nothing but a distraction, and all I've managed to do is screw everything up.

And piss Will off.

God, where is he?

When I finally get up the courage to leave the room, I see Dez outside the auditorium and run to him.

He grabs me and holds on tight.

I'm safe... for now.

"I'm so sorry, Rye," he says. "But you have plenty of other options."

"Tisch and Columbia, here we come." I squeeze back.

"That's right. You're too good for Guthrie anyway." He puts his arm around me. "Come on. It's almost time for the screenings."

This should be the greatest moment. Dez and I take our seats with the cast. The others try not to meet my eyes. Homer stands up at the front of the auditorium and thanks the organizers of the festival and the schools for their support.

"Now, without further ado," he says, "let's take a look at one of the films from this year's host school, my school, the Heights. This is *Alternate Realities* by Desmond Brandt."

I try to stay positive for Dez. This is his big moment. I smile at him and he puts my hand to his lips. It's work to concentrate when the film starts. My mind is racing.

Then it starts to really hit me. Dez's words echo in my head.

You belong in New York, Riley.

Why are you even bothering with Guthrie?

Don't waste your time on Guthrie.

The lights go up and the applause snaps me back. The audience is going crazy. Dez stands up with a quick wave and shy smile and Homer takes the stage again.

"The next nominated film is from Madison, Wisconsin. Please give a round of applause for *Misguided Youth* by Cody Miller."

The lights dim again. The various stories take up the screen, but I don't process any of them.

I don't like the way things are stacking up. Libby's accusations, even Stella's question: *Did Dez find your necklace? He was here.*

I now remember seeing Dez's camera bag backstage, before the festival.

Maybe he *has* been lying to me.

The lights go up and I race out of the auditorium. We don't have to be back here until the awards ceremony in the morning.

Dez chases me.

"Oh my God, oh my God." The realization is coming down on me all at once. "What did you do tonight, Dez?"

"What do you mean?" He looks panicked.

"What necklace were you looking for?"

"I don't know what you're talking about."

"You told Stella you were looking for my necklace. You were late. And you gave me the wrong time for my audition! What did you do, Dez?"

I don't like this. I don't like it one bit.

"Calm down, Riley." Dez holds up his hands. "It's not what you think."

I tremble.

"I know it looks bad," he says. "But I did it for you. All of it."

All of it? You ruined my clothes and shoes, too?

"You fucked up my entire audition!" I yell. "Why? Why would you do that?"

"Riley, you should be concentrating on Tisch, not Guthrie. Can we just get out of here? Go talk?"

I can't believe my ears. I feel so exposed. Naked. My heart hurts so much I can barely speak. "That wasn't for *you* to decide, Dez. Who the hell do you think you are?"

I'm too shocked to move or cry or yell or hit or break something. But I want to. In my head, I'm beating on his chest. I'm screaming. I'm bawling my eyes out.

By this time, a crowd is surrounding us. I see Stella out of the corner of my eye, trying to shoo them away.

Dez moves in again. "Let's go somewhere and talk," he says urgently. "Let me explain. Please. I'll make this up to you, I promise."

There's only one thing to do.

I walk right past him. Right up to Stella. "Think you could give me a ride?" I ask.

Her eyes are warm when she nods. "'Course." She flings her arm around me. "Let's get you out of here."

DEZ

"This is a chemical burn."

That's what Tyler Durden says in *Fight Club* as he pours lye on the narrator's hand. It's this deeply disturbing part in the movie when Tyler says that without pain and sacrifice, we would have nothing. It's something I used to believe. Something I now think is complete bullshit. Meanwhile, the narrator's skin melts right off the bone. Tyler Durden calls it premature enlightenment. He waits until the narrator can't take it anymore. Then he douses his hand with vinegar to neutralize the burn.

After Riley leaves with Stella, I wonder who will neutralize my burn. Everyone is glaring in my direction—everyone but Tori. She smirks and gives me a fake sympathy pat on the shoulder. Our cast and crew heard the whole thing. I can feel their contempt, disgust, anger, even pity, as well as the silent insults they're all hurling at me. One after another. As I walk to the guys' dressing room, everyone looks away and whispers. Even Jonah shakes his head at me.

I am officially scum. Worse than the dog crap you scrape off your shoe.

And I've hurt Riley.

I stomp out to the parking lot, open the car door, smash the flowers I got for Rye, and head home in silence.

She's gone.

This is *my* chemical burn.

There's only one way to salvage the mess I made, so I pick up the phone and make the call.

RILEY

Stella drives me home while I sit in shock. It's too much to process. I can actually feel my heart splitting wide open. The one person I loved and trusted the most has hurt me in the worst way.

Just breathe.

It's all I can do at the moment. Focus on the smallest of things. I'm suddenly so exhausted, I just want to sleep. To lose myself in my dreams. The pain is too much to take.

We pull up my driveway.

Stella puts her hand on my thigh but I can't feel it. It's like I'm not even in my own body.

"Do you want me to come in and sit with you for a while?" she asks in her soft voice.

I shake my head. "You've done so much already." I'm so thankful to her for getting me out of there. "I'm just going to go to sleep. It's been a shitty night."

She pats my leg. "Okay. But you can call me. Anytime."

I feel the tears prick my eyes, so I rush out of the car and give Stella a quick wave.

She jumps out after me.

"Oh, Rye," she calls out. "I got Will's records for you. Everyone was distracted, so I took the chance. I know this isn't a great time, but I thought you'd want them right away."

I turn around, take the paper, and shove it in my jacket.

DEZ

You would think that I would've tried harder to fight for my innocence and hold on to my lies when things went down that day. But when Riley looked into my eyes and demanded the truth, I guess I just couldn't fight against it anymore.

Looking back, I can see how messed up I was, but I wasn't so far gone that I didn't at least try to fix it. That was my first priority, I remember that much. My second? Coming clean to my parents. I'd screwed things up to such massive proportions that I couldn't undo it all on my own.

That night, *the* night, I sat them down and told them the whole story. Mom and Bernie sat and listened without moving, without saying a word. They just . . . listened.

They listened to my stories about ruining things with Riley's girlfriends and boyfriends and how I used Bernie to do it. They listened to my plan to get Riley to mess up during her Guthrie audition.

When I finished, Bernie stood up to talk. But, in a surprise move, Mom raised her hand as if to say *I got this.* That's when she finally grew a pair and went all military on my ass.

She laid out her own plan—and punishment—and there was no room for argument.

Those demands included: family therapy, a string of apologies, meetings with my guidance counselor, and a two-month grounding.

When she was done giving my sentence, she put her arms around me and said in my ear, "You need to make this right, Desmond."

RILEY

In the following weeks, I do my best to avoid Dez.

And Will.

Just as I thought it would, the report says Will was absent for three days after Ms. Dunn's murder.

He was gone the same amount of time after the film festival. And now he only shows up to school a few times a week. Not that *I've* seen him. If I still trusted Dez, I would have him help me talk to Bernie about reopening Ms. Dunn's case.

I even consider putting in an anonymous tip to the cops. But there's no way I can do that without getting Libby into trouble.

No, the only person I trust right now is Stella.

Every morning, she checks to see if Will showed up to class and then she texts me. I don't know which is worse, the days he shows up or the days he's gone.

I keep my sanity with homework, acting classes, and time at Java. When that isn't enough, I busy myself with internship applications for the summer and read every screenplay I can get my hands on.

As far as I can tell, Dez doesn't leave his house except for school. About a week after everything happened, he wrote me a letter. He tried to explain what he did and why. He begged for my forgiveness.

And I couldn't give it to him.

It didn't help that Libby wanted to have his balls for breakfast. Over time, she gathered the rest of the nasty details about how Dez had been sabotaging my relationships since sophomore year. Like a good friend, she forgave me for not believing her. And I forgave her, because that girl knows not what she does. Still, I can't let her in on my suspicions about Will.

As for the film, we won first place. Dez got a boatload of scholarship money. The rest of us made out pretty well too. I've used some of my award money to take classes at the Guthrie Theater. Dez and I made nice for the cause; we went through all the social events—the awards committee luncheon, the local newspaper interview, and the photo ops—as a happy team. It should've been the time of our lives. It wasn't.

After all, the one person I trusted more than anyone had somehow become my worst enemy.

But life goes on.

And it's going on without him.

The weeks roll by, like they do, and before I know it the holidays are upon us. And now *I'm* the one riddled with guilt. Especially for Mom and Dad. We had to cancel our annual Christmas brunch with Bernie, Trudy, and

Dez. My parents understand that I don't want to see Dez and they're siding with me, keeping a distance. But I know it's hurting them.

It's like my whole family is going through the break-up. We're all moving a bit slower than normal, our dinners have been quiet, and even the house seems down in the dumps.

"*You* are our priority," Dad says to me during dinner when I apologize again for Christmas brunch. "You need to do what's best for you, Riley. I'm still so mad at that boy. I just wish I could fix it. I wish I could take the pain away."

But we both know it's too late for that.

Too late for a lot of things.

Until I get a call from the Admissions office at Guthrie.

DEZ

We decide to have the last film club meeting on the day before the holiday break. The seniors are busy with college interviews and internships and they just want to be done with it. And the sophomores and juniors are anxiously waiting for the changing of the guard.

It's the end of an era.

By four o'clock, it's almost dark. The sky is purple as the snow comes down in heavy, wet flakes.

I'm still on the outs with the cast and crew, but it's my job to announce the director for next year's film. The seniors huddle in the front of the room and fill out their ballots. Riley won't even look at me. I've heard through the grapevine that she was accepted to Guthrie, early admission, and she's decided to go. But I checked online, and her audition spot is still open at Tisch. I hold out hope that she'll decide to go through with that audition. Then at least she'll have choices.

Stella collects all the ballots in a hat and passes it to me.

"Think she'll talk to me?" I ask her.

"I don't think she's there yet, Dez," Stella says. I can tell she's trying to be kind, but she seems genuinely freaked out by me.

Who could blame her.

"I never meant to hurt her," I say, but whether I'm trying to convince Stella or myself, I'm not sure.

"She knows that. Deep down, she knows."

"Do you think she'll ever forgive me?"

"I do," she says unconvincingly. "But not before you announce next year's director, so I think you better just count these ballots."

I take all the sheets of paper and unfold them. It's easy to tally the results. It's unanimous: Caleb will take my place next year.

Our time is over. I guess that's as it should be.

I make the announcement and the groups split up. The sophomores and juniors make plans and the seniors pack away all the equipment.

"Okay, guys, the first rule of film club is that we don't talk about film club," Caleb says to his new team.

That was my line.

We finish packing up and before I know it, we're done. I lose my nerve and don't try to talk to Rye. She's with Stella now, so I have no chance. The new film club has already left to celebrate, and the last of the seniors just walked out the door.

I go look at the edit suite one more time.

I wish I could edit my life and leave all the bad stuff

in here. The lies to Riley, messing up her audition, getting involved with Tori. All of it.

But I can't.

In the parking lot, the lights make all the white fluff sparkle. If Rye and I were walking together, we would've already had a snowball fight. We'd be laughing and yelling. Instead, the parking lot is eerie with silence.

I shuffle through the snow and that's when I see it.

That's when I know.

It's the shoes.

That was the clue I was looking for.

The footprints in front of me have an odd pattern—crisscrossing lines, like someone took a razorblade to them. I've seen this before.

In Bernie's crime scene photos. The footprints left in blood after Ms. Dunn's murder.

My ears grow warm and the back of my neck is itchy, and I know Rye was right all along. The killer has been here the entire time. At our school.

But who was it?

Who was out here tonight?

I go through a mental list of everyone I saw at school tonight—it's not a large group. It has to be someone we know, someone we know well. I speed up to a run and jump in my car.

I have to tell Riley.

RILEY

I'm thankful to be done—completely done—with the film club. I walk with Stella out to the parking lot. We're almost to her car when I hear it, the revving engine. To our left, there's a big black truck heading right for us.

"Watch out!" I scream, pushing Stella out of the way.

The truck whips past us into a spinning circle on the slippery snow. Will hangs out of his window and laughs.

"Merry Christmas, mother fuckers," he screams.

I freeze right there. I can't move. I haven't seen Will since the day of the festival. I'd hoped that he'd decided to let things be, but he's probably just been too busy filling holiday drug orders to bother me.

Marcus is walking to his car, but he stops to wave at Will. He laughs and shakes his head.

Yes, he would think Will's stunt was funny.

"Don't worry, Riley." Stella grabs my hand and leads me to her car. "He's not going to do anything with people around."

She's right.

Stella gives me a ride home and we make plans to see each other over break. I couldn't be happier to have the time off.

I walk up the driveway and notice Bernie's police cruiser parked next door. It's times like this when I'm thankful to live next to a cop.

I go into the dark house and flip on the lights. There's an open bottle of wine and two wine glasses sitting on the counter. Mom and Dad must've gotten some good news.

The note on the table confirms it. Dad gets to add another class next semester, so they went out to celebrate. Finally, something to be happy about.

I'm exhausted, so I grab a blanket and curl up on the couch. I try to sleep but my head is pounding. When I can't take it anymore, I walk into the kitchen for some Advil.

The door is wide open, flapping in the breeze.

Looks like I forgot to shut the door.

I close it and reach for the Advil in the cabinet above the fridge.

Before I can grab it, a sharp, debilitating pain shoots through my head and down my neck, and then everything goes black.

DEZ

My fingertips are raw and my nails are bitten down to the quick. I've been chewing them since I found the footprints. I have to tell Riley that Ms. Dunn's killer is still here. Rye was right.

She was right about a lot of things.

I take a deep breath as I head over to her house—I know she doesn't want to see me, but I have to find a way to make her listen.

One foot in front of the other, Dez.

I make it around to the back and see shadows float across the windows. Looks like I might have an audience for this. I swing around to the door. It's wide open. Without thinking, I walk in.

Inside, it's quiet … too quiet.

Something's not right here, and I suddenly feel like I've been punched in the gut. I take slow steps toward the living room. "Riley?" I call out. "Are you there? Rye?"

My words are cut off by a python that's wrapped itself around my neck.

No. This can't be happening.

I'm trapped in a chokehold.

But not for long. I'm not going to go down like this.

I feel the python's breath on my neck.

"Desmond. Fucking. Brandt," a familiar voice hisses. "You're not supposed to be here tonight."

My head tries to place the voice of this asshole while my body squirms in his grip, searching for a way out of the hold. "Where is she? Where's Riley?"

"You fucking idiot. You have no idea what you just walked into. You've made a huge mistake, friend. Huge."

What has he done with her?

Reaching around my neck, I feel my way to his head. He must be wearing a ski mask—I grab a handful of hair through it and pull, jerking his skull from side to side.

"I wouldn't do that if I were you," he says.

"Let me go, asshole, or I swear to God, I'll kill you."

"Funny, that's exactly what I was thinking."

I'm able to get a grip on his neck and I lock in. I flip him around my body and when I do, his feet fly out from under him. And there they are.

The shoes.

It's the killer. It has to be.

But why is he here?

He recovers and slams me against the counter. Still, I advance, pulling back my arm and clenching my fist.

I connect with his masked face, and can tell by his eyes

that my connection was good. I lean across him, dropping my weight on his chest.

"Riley," I call out again. "Riley, it's okay, I've got him."

I try to pull the ski mask off but the guy is wild—he shakes his head and tries to buck me off.

You're going to have to do better than that.

I tighten my grip and almost have the mask off. But in moments, my arms fall away—there's an explosion in my head. When I look up, the asshole is holding a bottle of wine.

I'm falling, reaching for him to steady myself. I grab hold of the back of his mask. It slides down to the floor with me.

I see his face.

Oh, shit.

That's the last thing I remember before he strikes me with the bottle again.

RILEY

When I come to, I feel the painful pounding deep in my skull. I'm sprawled out on Dad's leather recliner, desperate to see what's going on around me. It hurts to move. I reach up to feel my head and realize my hands are taped together. I run them through my hair—it's wet and sticky. I'm stiff, so I try to stretch my legs but they're taped together too. I open my eyes and see more tape around my middle, securing me to the chair. I blink, over and over again, until I can focus. Though the room is dim, I can still make out a figure in the chair across from me.

I try to scream, but it comes out strained and hoarse. Dez shakes his head.

Oh my God. What the hell is going on?

"Don't say anything," he whispers. "Everything is going to be okay." His eyes dart around the room and I feel like I'm going to throw up.

He sits there, not moving. His eyes meet mine. They narrow like he's trying to tell me something.

"Why are you doing this, D—? "

Before the words are even out, I see that Dez is also tied to the chair.

I let out a silent cry that ripples through my body.

In the shadows, another figure appears.

A boy I know.

Marcus.

"Let her go, Marcus," Dez says, thrashing in his chair.

Marcus backhands Dez and a loud crack echoes in the room. "I told you. No talking."

Dez's face reddens and his lip starts to bleed.

"Next time, I do it to her," he says.

DEZ

"You really fucked this up, Desmond." Marcus paces around the living room. My eyes don't meet his. I focus on Riley. Her face is pale and her head is bleeding. I can see her hands shake. I try to calm her with my eyes, but she no longer trusts me.

My heart squeezes at the thought.

"It's Riley I want, not you," Marcus says. "Shit." He runs his gloved hand through his hair—back and forth.

My eyes move to him now and I take him in. He's wearing a leather jacket and jeans. The ski mask sticks out of his back pocket and he holds a huge pair of scissors down by his side.

Stop.

Rewind.

Again, my eyes move down his body to the scissors.

Pause.

I close my eyes and see Ms. Dunn's crime scene photo again. I see the printed report. The report I shouldn't have been looking at.

Multiple stab wounds to the victim's torso.

Wounds measure one inch in length.

I open my eyes, back to the scissors, and realize Marcus is holding the murder weapon.

I pray Rye doesn't see it.

What does he want with her?

"So, Riley," Marcus says. "I suppose Emma's already been to see you. Hmm?"

Riley doesn't move, but I see her eyes travel down to the scissors in his hand. Her eyes are full of horror and I see her swallow.

"I asked you a question, you little dyke!"

Riley shudders. "No," she squeaks out. "Emma hasn't been here."

"It seems she wants you back." He flicks the scissors at her.

"No." Riley shakes her head.

"Don't lie, Riley." Marcus' eyes are wild, scanning the doors and windows. "I really hate liars. You know she dumped me for you."

Rye shakes her head again.

"Oh, yes she did. Things were going great, and then she dumps me out of the blue. Says she can't be without you. What a lying tease. You're all the same."

He moves closer to Rye and my adrenaline kicks in. I pull at the duct tape, but it just digs into my skin. "Who are all the same?" I ask, trying to divert his attention.

Come over here, asshole.

"Women, Dez." He laughs but his hand is shaking. "They tease and lie."

"Yes." I try to keep him talking, keep him from moving toward Rye. "Yes, they do. Why? Who else teased you?"

"Rachel." He laughs again. "That'd be Ms. Dunn to you. Or, *was* Ms. Dunn. Yeah, dude, I had the hots for teacher."

Riley lets out a whimper. I will her to keep quiet but she lets out another.

Now she's done it.

Marcus flashes Riley a warning glare and then looks back at me.

"And she was hot for me," he continues. "Well, she was before she got cold feet. Just like Emma. But you know"—Marcus stalks over to Riley, this time waving the scissors in front of her face—"I did learn something from that brief love affair."

I endure his story. I hear his words, but they become muffled and sound almost as if he's underwater. It's because my mind is drifting, going into protection mode. I see the murder scene play out in front of me. One element at a time.

Marcus' gloved hands.

The blades of the scissors. Opening and closing. Opening and closing. They let out that squeaky sound, whining for something to cut.

"See," Marcus goes on. "*I* was the only one who suffered when I killed Rachel. She didn't know any better. She was dead. And I was left living without her. Seeing her face wherever I went. It was a stupid move on my part. This time I won't be as foolish."

I feel a faint sense of relief. At least he doesn't plan on killing us.

"Yeah," he adds. "Instead of killing Emma, I'll kill the person she loves the most."

I cough, choking on my own saliva. I'm going to be sick.

"If you're gone, Riley, then it's Emma who'll suffer. But she'll get over it... and I'll be waiting when she does. I can be very patient."

At this point, it's clear. This is not a stunt. He came here for one reason: to kill Riley. My mind races, searching for something, trying to form a plan. I can't think. I can't do anything. I'm stuck. Impotent. Weak. I'm helpless and I start to slip away. My eyes get fuzzy, like it's a dream sequence in a movie.

A new song begins to play in my head. My soundtrack has switched from Chris Isaak to Stealers Wheel's "Stuck in the Middle with You"—the song in that twisted ear-cutting scene from *Reservoir Dogs.* I'm caught up in a fucking Quentin Tarantino movie.

I break out of it. The fuzziness gives way and Marcus comes back into focus. Still, I hear Stealers Wheel, singing about an eerie feeling that something isn't right.

Marcus is poking the side of his leg with the scissors. It's like he's in a trance, keeping time with the music in my head.

Then he looks at me and shakes his head. "You, my friend, are a victim of being in the wrong place at the wrong time." He lets out a little chuckle, turns his back on me, and stalks over to Riley. I squirm and twist my body, trying to loosen my bindings. They only cut deeper into my wrists and ankles.

I close my eyes and flip back to *Reservoir Dogs* playing in my mind. The infamous Mr. Blonde commands the screen. He walks across the warehouse—the hideout for a bunch of thugs after a robbery goes bad. Mr. Blonde has taken a police officer hostage. The cop sits bound to a chair—much like I am right now. Blonde turns on the radio. "Stuck in the Middle with You" is ringing through the speakers.

Mr. Blonde's next movements are set to the music, perfectly. He lifts his black cowboy boot and rests it on a chair. His hand reaches inside the boot and pulls out a switchblade. He opens it slowly and runs it along his five o'clock shadow. Mr. Blonde is intimate with the blade—just like Marcus is with his metal shears.

Mr. Blonde sings along with the words, dances to the tune, while the cop struggles in his chair. Again, like me.

Mr. Blonde then rips a piece of duct tape from the roll and slowly wraps it around the cop's mouth. He's calm and cool as can be when he leans over the cop and says he's going to torture him.

I stop the movie in my mind and order my eyes to open. They land on Marcus. He's talking to Riley. A deep red pattern blooms on his pant leg, from his jabs with the scissors.

The fucked-up song about losing control continues in my head, a fitting track for the real-life nightmare playing out in front of me.

"Marcus," I yell. "Marcus."

He leaves us and dashes into the kitchen. Riley squeezes her eyes shut.

"Rye," I beg. "Rye!" I need her to look at me. We're running out of time.

In seconds, Marcus is back. I stare into his eyes but they're vacant now. He's looking right through me.

"Marcus," I stutter as the panic courses through my veins. Behind my eyelids, I see Mr. Blonde take his blade to the cop's ear.

He begins slicing.

The camera jerks to the ceiling but I can hear it.

I hear it all.

The struggle and pain and... torture.

The camera moves back to Mr. Blonde. He's now holding the cop's ear he just hacked off with the switchblade. He flips it around in his hand. The cop screams and groans.

In the real world, the room spins. *Fuck, can this be the real world?*

Yes, it can. It is.

But then Quentin Tarantino takes the reins. He takes over this real world. He takes over my *life*.

Desmond Brandt Death Scene:
Take one.

DEZ continues to look at RILEY. The camera moves back and forth between them in uneasy, choppy movements. The song "Stuck in the Middle with You" continues to play.

CUT TO:

CLOSE UP: DEZ

DEZ'S eyes water. He's shaking, pleading with MARCUS. The camera pulls out, framing the profiles of DEZ and MARCUS.

DEZ
Please. Don't do this. Don't do it, man.

TAKE AUDIO FULL:

SONG PLAYS: Please.... Please...

MARCUS
Sorry, Dez. I have no other option.

In a flash, MARCUS' hand is at DEZ'S face. MARCUS pulls down DEZ'S bottom lip, cranks open his mouth, and stuffs a dishrag inside. DEZ chokes and gags. We watch as his body shudders.

DEZ lets out a gasp and Riley explodes in sobs.

RILEY

Groans escape from Dez. They start deep in his throat but are stifled by the dishtowel stuffed in his mouth. His guttural pleas rise and fall. Everything inside me tightens.

It is the most frightening sound I've ever heard.

I stop moving, stop breathing. I can't take anymore. I just want it all to end. Marcus stands in front of me now, holding a pair of old metal shears to my throat. And that's when the flashbacks come.

A timeline begins to develop…

Last year, Marcus was always waiting in the wings any time I went to Ms. Dunn's classroom to talk. I can still see the strange looks he'd give me when I left her room. Angry. Possessive. Unsettling.

And during her prayer service, he was totally on edge. He was a ticking time bomb, picking fights and talking shit. Just waiting for someone to do something to justify his wrath.

How did I not see it?

I remember the way he interrupted me when I was looking

at the film footage from the day of her murder. And the way he touched her statues the day Homer brought them to me.

My reverie ends when I feel the blade of the scissors touch my skin. It's cold and heavy. Marcus tests it, running the pointy tip down from the hollow under my ear, along my neck, to my shoulder.

Dez groans.

The blade takes little bites as Marcus varies the pressure in the movement. The open skin burns when the air hits it.

My eyes stay on Dez. I try to talk to him with my eyes. He continues to struggle, continues to fight. I try to tell him it's okay. I'm glad Marcus moved to me first. I couldn't stand to watch him hurt Dez, no matter what's happened between us.

Marcus pulls the scissors away and, out of the corner of my eye, I can see him change his grip. I hold my breath and I get lost in Dez's eyes again. *This is it.* My mind flashes to my parents. To Ms. Dunn. To …

A person springing forward in the darkness … someone who takes a glass vase and clubs Marcus in the head.

He drops to the floor—just a few measly feet in front of me.

My eyes adjust to the surroundings while my brain tries to make sense of it all. Soon I can make out our savior.

It's Stella.

Then it all happens so fast, I can barely keep up. There are voices and movement all around me, but all I can think about is Marcus almost killing us. Just like he did to Ms. Dunn. Beautiful, amazing Ms. Dunn.

In my mind, I see him with the scissors. Stabbing her. Watching the life drain from her.

My breath hitches and the tears flow. He was here the whole time.

I feel like I'm sinking.

Until I focus on Stella.

She doesn't let up. As Marcus lies on the floor, Stella smashes the vase on his head again—this time so hard that it shatters everywhere. Rivers of blood flow down his face, pooling on the floor. He lies still.

I smell the rusty stench of his blood and my head goes foggy. Then there's a cold blade at my wrist as Stella uses the scissors to cut me free.

I rub my wrists, still paralyzed in my seat.

Stella moves to release Dez, and he's at my side in an instant.

"We've got to get out of here, Riley." He's trying to yell, but he's hoarse. He and Stella each take one of my arms and we all run out of the house.

Then Dez is gone.

Seconds later, he's with Bernie, running across the lawn.

"Get the girls inside, Dez," Bernie says, rushing into my house in full PD mode.

Trudy holds open the door and we run in.

"Holy fuck, Stella." Dez is staring at her in awe. "You're Orange, man. You're better than Mr. Orange."

Dez stumbles around; he must be in shock or something. Trudy helps him sit down. He puts his head between his legs, trying to get his bearings.

Stella raises her eyebrows. She's just as messed up as me and Dez.

"Mr. Orange is the hero in *Reservoir Dogs*," I tell her. "He saved the cop—at least for a while." I'm rambling. "It's the highest compliment Dez could ever give."

Trudy moves to my side and settles me on the couch as well. She strokes my hair and holds me and Dez, rocking us like she did when we were little.

I let her.

As my head finally begins to clear, I have a terrible thought.

Emma.

What if he hurt her too?

Stella looks at me and I whisper, "Emma."

"On it." Stella gently touches my arm and steps away, quickly hitting the keys on her phone.

I sit there on Dez's couch, rocking back and forth. Dez takes the blanket from the arm of the sofa and wraps me in it. He's shaking. Trudy is now at the window, both guarding us from the danger and waiting for a sign from Bernie.

Stella gets off her phone, crouches down in front of me, and puts a hand to my cheek. "She's okay, Riley. Emma is fine." I drop my head to her shoulder and she holds me. "You're okay, Rye. Everything is going to be okay now."

We sit there in silence until the sirens ring out from every direction. A man's voice barks orders outside, and men in uniform move across the Brandts' yard. As I get up to get a better look, Trudy shoos me away.

“Don’t even think about it,” she says, pointing back to the couch. “Sit.”

We sit for what seems like hours until Trudy whispers, “Oh, thank God.”

And I know Bernie is safe.

This time, Dez and Stella join me as I move toward the window. There must be a dozen cops swarming around. They part down the middle as two men move a gurney out my front door.

It’s Marcus.

The EMTs push him into an ambulance and two police officers jump in the back to stand guard.

He’s caught. It’s finally over.

Maybe everything will be okay now.

I wish I could feel relief, but I don’t.

All I have left are questions.

I start peppering Stella with them. “How did you know? Why did you come?”

She looks at Dez and smiles. “Dez figured it out. He saw the same footprints in the parking lot today that were in Bernie’s crime photos. Since he knew you wouldn’t take his calls, he called me on the way to your house—and when I couldn’t get ahold of you, I had a bad feeling. I came as fast as I could.”

A feeling? A feeling saved us?

“I didn’t know *who* the killer was, at first,” Dez says. “I just knew he goes to our school. If I knew he’d come after you, Rye, I would’ve called Bernie right away.” Dez rests his head on his fist. “I’m so *sorry*.”

I never heard a word sound so heavy. I meet his eyes now because I know.

I know how sorry he is.

DEZ

INT. BERNIE'S OFFICE—NIGHT

DESMOND sneaks into BERNIE'S office once again. He begins typing on BERNIE'S computer and stops when he finds MARCUS' rap sheet. He reads it and moves on to the file that says "Notes." These are the notes from the attack at the Frost house. Then he finds the quotes from people brought in for questioning.

DESMOND reads through the night.

Once all the questioning is done and the PD is getting ready to close the case, I hack into Bernie's files once again, to read all about the guy who killed Ms. Dunn. The boy who wanted to kill Riley. Who almost killed me. I find out that since Marcus Flynn was eighteen when he killed Ms. Dunn and held me and Riley captive, he'll be tried as an adult when the case goes to trial.

I discover that Marcus' parents are divorced. I look over his school tests scores—he's smart, really smart. I read testimony from people who called him a liar and a cheat. People who describe him as controlling and intense.

They could just as easily be describing me.

I learn that Marcus had a pattern of violence with the girls he dated. Never enough to send him away or get him in any real trouble, but a pattern that escalated.

So many of his crimes were secret for a long time.

Again, like me.

The moment is like a slap in the face, a kick in the balls. It's a jolt out of a dream. A shock, a surprise. A wake-up call. A realization.

I sob.

Hard, snotty cries that haven't come from me since I was a kid. I'm afraid that because I've finally released them, I'll never stop. I keep seeing Riley beaten, bound, and terrified. In some way, I feel like I put her there with Marcus.

I wonder how far I would've gone to control her. How many more times would I have fucked things up for her?

Am I really any better than Marcus?

I'm not sure I'm strong enough to hear the answer. I'm not sure I want to know.

RILEY

Fast-Forward: Two Weeks.

It's weird, but having a near-death experience with someone doesn't necessarily bring you closer together. It's not like the movies, where you have this life-affirming moment, where nothing else matters but the two of you and a second chance at life.

It's not for me and Dez, anyway.

It's the opposite, really. For me, being so close to death only made me more careful... especially about who I'll let into my life again. *Me.* My choice. My decision. I finally realize that I have that control.

After the attack, Marcus went to the hospital. His injuries were minor, so he was locked up the same night. He hasn't seen the light of day since and won't for a long time.

Mom and Dad immediately removed all evidence of that night from our home. Still, I can see him there in the living room. I can feel him in the hallway. I can hear him in the kitchen.

Over these past few weeks, my parents have stuck to me like a postage stamp. I can't even go pee by myself. They don't budge, no matter how I try to lighten up the whole almost-getting-murdered thing. They hover and smother me during the day and keep vigil by my bed at night.

I'm thankful.

Especially during the nights filled with nightmares—when I relive the attack over and over again. Or, when I stay up trying to make sense of it all—or worse, wondering what it was like for Ms. Dunn.

How many times did Marcus stab Ms. Dunn before she died?

Did she beg for her life?

Did she know why he did it?

Was she in terrible pain?

Now that it's all over, all I'm left with is time. To think. Really think. It didn't take long for the anger to simmer down. It's not boiling over anymore at all. It's just tepid water.

It's now that I begin to miss my friend.

Dez.

Still, I know it's a pain I have to endure, and one that he'll have to face too. And I'm truly sorry for that.

As for Emma, I'm happy to report that things have finally become normal with us. She still hasn't come out to her mom—I didn't expect her to. But I have faith that she will. When she's ready. Things have settled down at school, too. Most everyone has stopped gawking at me in the halls and Tori's even started harassing me with her snide comments during gym. I almost feel at home again.

Before I know it, it's time for the New York auditions—for both me and Dez.

The day I'm supposed to leave, I have lunch near the airport with Libby, Emma, and Stella. We talk and laugh and stuff our faces with the best pizza in Minneapolis.

When Libby and Emma head out, Stella moves closer.

"I thought they'd never leave," she says, giving me those goose bumps again.

We stay there for another hour, until we can't delay anymore.

"Let's get you to the airport," she says.

"Yep, it's time," I agree.

We get up and she puts her hand in mine.

DEZ

Ever since the fiasco at the film festival, I've done everything Mom asked and then some. Don't get me wrong—even after my awakening, it doesn't come easy. For a long time, I still let myself believe that I was only trying to help Rye. It's funny, though, how clear things become when you're alone.

After Marcus was arrested and I'd made all my apologies, I thought things would go back to the way they were.

It didn't work out that way.

Then, right when I thought I was going to lose it, really lose it, Jonah finally came around. He invited me to one of his youth group deals. I hate that shit and he knows it, but I took the olive branch and didn't let go. I was desperate.

I've been going with him for the past month. I'm not all Zen now, or perfect, or even close. But I'm better than I was.

I hope Riley is too.

I wait at the Humphrey terminal. Right after we got our invitations, Rye and I bought cheapo tickets to JFK on Sun Country Airlines. I haven't checked in yet. Instead,

I wait at Caribou Coffee and drink a dark roast loaded with cream. Despite everything that's happened, I hold out hope that Riley's changed her mind. Who knew I'd become an optimist?

The clock continues to click toward 2:10 p.m. Our departure time. I stay as long as I can.

She's not coming.

I should've known. I guess this is how the story is supposed to end. Still, I don't want to leave without her. I don't want this to be it.

I feel like Rocky Balboa. I'm beat and battered and all I want is my girl…

"Adrian!" Rocky screams over and over at the end of the film. "Adrian!"

Adrian pushes through the crowd, trying to get to Rocky, and when she does, they lock in an embrace.

I am Rocky, and in my mind I scream, "Riley! Riley! Riley!"

People rush all around me, trying to get home, trying to leave. It's a buzz of farewells and welcome backs.

But I never get my embrace, because Riley never shows.

RILEY

Stella and I sit in her car in the parking lot at Fort Snelling, where we can see the parade of planes coming and going. I try to predict which one Dez is on.

"Are you sure you made the right decision?" she asks. "There's still time. You could still go to the Tisch audition and then make up your mind later. A backup, just in case."

"That's what this is." I rest my head on her shoulder. "Coming out here to say goodbye to Dez was my backup plan. I needed to make sure I was doing the right thing. I wanted to give myself the option of a harried airport scene, if I wanted it."

"And do you?" Stella asks.

I shake my head. "Not in the slightest."

"And what about Dez?" She lowers her voice. "Any second thoughts there?"

"Hmmm," I say, feeling the squeeze in my chest. "Yeah, tons of second thoughts. Like... did I drive him to the craziness? Could I have prevented it? Was it my fault?"

"No, no, and no." Stella's face is tight; she's clenching her teeth.

"Yeah, I know you're right. But it's hard. He was my friend for so long, and to have it end like this . . . "

"It doesn't have to be the end, Rye. Not if you don't want it to be."

"It does." I take an extra gulp of air to keep the tears from falling. "I could never trust him again, and I don't want to live that way. Not anymore."

"I get it. But maybe in time?"

"Maybe."

"Well." Stella scoots over and puts her hands on my shoulders. "There's plenty of time for maybes, but let's just enjoy right now. You're going to the U of M, Riley. Your Guthrie dream is coming true."

It's strange to think of it as *my* dream. It had always been *ours*. Dez and I each had half—it was only together that we made a whole. I ache for him; a phantom pain of a former life. It hurts, sometimes more than I can bear. Then at other times, I'm relieved that old me—that old us—is gone.

A plane soars above now and as we watch it go overhead, I say a silent goodbye to Dez.

Stella stays close. She is one of those people who never has to be in control. She's content to just be.

She leans in and gives me the softest of kisses on my cheek.

My face stings from her lips.

It's a good sting.

The best.

FINAL SCENE

It's time. The final scene. One of the most important things in a film. A great ending can make a movie. Look at *Pulp Fiction*, or *Silence of the Lambs*, or—and I can't believe I'm going to say this—*Say Anything*.

I was so hoping this story would have a Hollywood ending—all sappy and sweet, wrapped in a nice big red bow.

Just the way Riley likes 'em

But it wasn't meant to be. I guess I jumped the shark after all.

I still think about Riley every day. Sometimes I catch myself ready to call her after I see an awesome film or learn something cool in class. Then I remember that I don't even have her number anymore.

How's that for a happy ending?

There are so many great last lines in the movies. So many we could use here.

I could take Scarlett O'Hara's last line in *Gone with the Wind:* "I'll go home, and I'll think of some way to get him back! After all, tomorrow is another day!" A few word changes and it would be perfect for the end of our story.

Or we could end with a meeting between me and Riley and steal from another classic, *Casablanca*, where Bogart says, "Louis, I think this is the beginning of a beautiful friendship." Yeah, what I wouldn't do to be friends with Rye again.

But more apropos would be a dark ending. Something like the ending in *Sunset Boulevard:* "You see, this is my life. It always will be! There's nothing else. Just us, and the cameras, and those wonderful people out there in the dark. All right, Mr. DeMille, I'm ready for my close-up."

Forget it.

Here's the real shit: I no longer care about modeling my life after a film. For so long, I wished I could edit out all the bad stuff that happened. But I'm not so sure anymore. That time in my life was a big part of me—of who I was and what I was.

And Rye? Well, she'll never be gone. Not completely. After all, she's my childhood, my history, my home.

Yeah, my life is no movie. Who are we kidding? But just for grins, this would be my closing scene: A college freshman in an edit suite at Columbia going over the footage for a documentary.

The film I'm working on has taken on a life of its own, *without* me directing it. A piece about . . . love.

Sort of a tribute to Riley.

I shuttle through interviews of people talking about love. Gay love. Straight love. Romantic love. Platonic love. You get the idea.

And as you listen to the people talk, it's clear.

Love is simple and complicated and easy and hard. People do great and terrible things all in the name of it. Love, to use a cliché, makes the world go round.

But mostly, love is honest. It has to be.

And that, my friends, is a wrap.

Cue the music... roll the credits.

Maris Ehlers Photography

About the Author

Dawn Klehr began her career in TV, and though she's been on both sides of the camera, she prefers to be behind the lens. Mostly she loves to get lost in stories—in film, in the theater, or on the page—and she's a sucker for both the sinister and the sappy. She's currently channeling her dark side as she works on her next book.

Dawn lives in the Twin Cities with her funny husband, adorable son, and naughty dog. *The Cutting Room Floor* is her debut YA novel. Visit her online at DawnKlehr.blogspot.com.